THE ORPHAN'S HOPE

SADIE HOPE

JOIN MY NEWSLETTER

Nora woke as she had every day since Valeria left her, with a sheen of fine sweat on her forehead and the hammering of her heart against the bars of her ribcage. She knew, as she always knew, that she had been dreaming something dreadful, but all knowledge of what it was faded in the cold grey light of a London dawn, leaving only the dread behind.

The room was cold, the loose-fit and grubby window had been struck by a bird or a stone, leaving a long and jagged line from corner to corner and a teardrop-shaped hole in the dead middle. A new pane would cost money, so Miss June had left the window un-mended.

Nora grabbed the small rag from where it had fallen beside the pallet and pushed it back into the hole. It must have fallen out overnight and let the cold damp air in.

Sophie snarled something incoherent at her from the pallet and tugged back some of the ragged covers. Sophie had gathered the younger girls about her for warmth, pushing Nora closer to the window in the night.

As the orphanage took on more mouths and Miss June found more ways to stretch the small donations and government shillings further and further the house's dilapidation was beginning to show more starkly. Not that Miss June seemed to benefit much by the profits she squeezed from the human traffic she arranged. Nora was sure the old witch was angrier and unhappier than ever.

Nora was also sure that an unhappy Miss June would mean unhappier times for all of them.

Sophie still lay there with her eyes closed. Though by her breathing Nora could tell that she too was awake and waiting for the bell that would summon them to break their fast and say their prayers. Miss

June had also discovered religion since Valeria had left. Hers was not a nice faith, not encouraging but she preached a wrathful God. It seemed to make her happy to think that God would strike them down for their laziness or slovenly ways.

Nora wondered what Valeria would have thought and for a moment a dark despair came over her. How she missed her friend. Sometimes she was even jealous but she had to cling to the thought that if Valeria could make it out, so could she.

The cold air seemed thick with the tension of the day to come. The cloud cover wouldn't give away any clues what time it was, but Nora always woke just a few minutes before the bell, so it must be soon, she thought.

She watched Sophie curled up among the younger girls — some as young as nine or ten, though most were guessing by how many winters they could remember — Sophie and herself were among the oldest left in Miss June's care.

When Valeria left, Sophie had looked to persecute someone else and Nora had at first been the target of her hate. Nora had instead put her efforts into looking after the younger girls, and Sophie had turned to tormenting them instead. The result was an uneasy alliance between the two girls.

The bell rang and with a sudden flurry of motion, Sophie rose to her feet, ripping the covers off the younger girls. Nudging them awake with a rough shove of her feet. One girl, who was a little slower to come to, received a firm kick to her behind.

Before the bell's tones had faded away, Sophie was haranguing them out into the narrow hall. They trudged to another room, with a bucket of water and piles of dirty clothes. They quickly dressed, packed in, and moved slowly towards the dining hall.

Miss June stood at the end of the hall pinching ears and dispensing the day's tasks. This girl to the kitchens to light the fires.

"Be sure not to use too much coal."

This girl to the dining room to scrub the tables.

"Cleanliness is next to Godliness," her voice barked. Others were told to mop floors, or wipe windows, or draw water from the pump. Some would even start on the laundry and mending that Miss June took in to supplement her income.

Nora lowered her gaze the closer she got to the front of the queue, she could feel Sophie close to her and wanted to get away from the mean girl.

She heard Miss June give away the last of the real jobs. Damn, Nora thought, they had been too slow. It would be work of Miss June's own invention for them. The group of girls in front of her were given the task of scraping the soot out of the grate in Miss June's small apartments in the back of the orphanage.

Nora felt like a mouse under the eye of a cat as her turn came.

"What's this?" snapped Miss June to Sophie. "Your clothes are filthy, both of you are to get washed before you start your chores."

Nora looked up. Sophie's ragged old outfit was no filthier than the scraps Miss June had clothed the rest of them in.

"You and Nora can do the laundry before you eat."

Nora's heart sank. Laundry was normally a job

assigned after breakfast. One that would take hours and required not just hard work, but cold work.

The younger girls were set to sweeping out the bedrooms while Nora and Sophie walked back down the corridor to the small bathroom with its copper bucket for their weekly wash, and its large pile of dirty garments.

Breakfast would be served and eaten by the time they had moved all this to the cask outside. She looked at Sophie, whose pretty golden locks had lost much of their shine, and at her own hands which shook with cold and malnourishment already.

The thought struck her very suddenly and with crystal clarity. If I do not leave this place, I will die here.

She wouldn't be the first. Cold had taken many a girl. Hunger too. Cholera had swept through an orphanage in Whitechapel just a few weeks ago and the owners of the orphanage had been ruined by the cost of paying for burials for the bodies.

Miss June had spent a full week eyeing them all up suspiciously and at the first sign of weakness or paleness — both common in her girls — she would begin to tut to herself and mutter, "Small girls, small graves."

There were tears in Sophie's eyes as she looked at her dress. "It's not fair," she muttered. Then repeated it louder as if convincing herself. "It's not fair."

"No," said Nora. "It's not. But we do what we must." Her own voice was trembling. She started to pile up the clothes onto a blanket she could use to wrap them up in.

The sun was a glowing patch of cloud directly overhead when they hung up the last of the clothes on the line in the yard of the orphanage building. Nora's fingers, already sore from the days of needlework Miss June still had them do, were cramped up into arthritic claws. Her skin was wrinkled from working the wet clothes, calloused by the rough cloth, and torn from the clumsiness that came from being cold and hungry.

Sophie's feet were similarly wrecked by trampling the clothes in the icy water of the wash tub. They had said hardly a word to each other all morning, the dead silence hanging between them seemed, after a while, to be a third presence in their chore, a shadow that meant them ill. But neither had the strength to open their mouth and chase the silence away from its haunting vigil.

The dining room had been converted over to a workshop by the time they arrived. The other girls sat in rows sewing away by hand at the small battered table.
Miss June paced up and down among them, her eyes shining with a febrile light.

"Please, Miss June. Might I eat something before we begin?" Sophie asked her.

"You wicked child. You have wasted the morning drawing out your work and now you wish to eat food that I must pay for. When you have sewed your share and contributed a little towards your keep, then you may have your bowl of soup."

Nora saw Sophie's shoulders fall and didn't bother to even try and appeal on their behalves to the old harpy. She sat down with Sophie on the end of the table. Miss June piled a small collection of cotton dresses in front of them. The dresses were clean and soft, no fancier than the wife of a factory worker might wear, but luxurious to Nora's eyes.

She tried to un-flex her cold hands and rub some warmth into them, but the room was no warmer than the yard had been. Her fingers wouldn't close on the needle and it slipped from her grasp.

Out of nowhere Miss June's hand slapped hers. "What are you playing at, Nora? Get to work."

"But, Miss June." She felt a heavy cough rise in her throat.

"No 'buts', you lazy child. Set to."

"I did the same work and can still sew Miss June," Sophie whispered and flashed Nora a sneer but it lacked any real conviction or joy in its cruelty. "I don't see why she should make such a fuss."

"See child, you will not avoid your duties to God and to me by playing this foolish game."

Nora reached for her needle, dropped it. Tried again, dropped it again. The cough ripped out of her, hurting her chest and making her see stars.

The world seemed so dark around her, and she was so tired.

Her chest hurt, or was cold, or both. There was a deep hard nothing right in the core of her. It was getting harder to tell what she felt.

Had the sun gone out? she wondered. It was so dark.

With a feeling of desperation, she searched, trying to find her needle, but it seemed hidden in the moving surface of the table. Miss June was just a dark silhouette hanging over her. The rest of the girls had faded completely from sight.

Miss June's shadow fell on her, blotting out the last few shimmers of light, and Nora was lost without a sense of sound, or touch, or of up or down.

Floating in a nothingness, she was alone with one thought, *this must be death.*

CHAPTER TWO

*V*aleria smiled contentedly as she passed the cloth over the library shelf. Removing just a speck of dust before replacing the three volumes of *Capital* and two of *An Inquiry into the Nature and Causes of the Wealth of Nations* on the now spotless surface. With a smile on her face she pulled out the next few books along, Malthus, Fleetwood, Canard, set them on the shelf below and swept the rag through the dust once more.

Once before she had tried to read some of these books, opening one up at random, but she had been faced with sentences like:

Within the capitalist system all methods for raising the social productiveness of labour are brought about at the cost of the individual labourer; all means for the development of production transform themselves into means of domination over, and exploitation of, the producers; they mutilate the labourer into a fragment of a man, degrade him to the level of an appendage of a machine, destroy every remnant of charm in his work and turn it into a hated toil; they estrange from him the intellectual potentialities of the labour process in the same proportion as science is incorporated in it as an independent power...

The words had seemed to go on and on in the same vein until she was ready to fall off her chair with boredom. Worse than that, none of it had made any sense to her at all. This didn't stop her smiling and singing softly to herself. The library was her favourite part of the house.

Across the room, were the great works of biology, art, and history. These thrilled her whenever she tentatively dipped into them. On the other side was a vast wall of fiction. In this she could lose days, if only the dusting weren't keeping her busy.

Nora's stories had kept her alive in Miss June's orphanage. That and the ones they made up of a better life. For a moment she wondered about her friend. How was she doing? How she longed to see her. Several times she had gone back to the orphanage but each time she had been chased away. The last time Miss June had told her that Nora would be sent to the workhouse if she called again. That her presence was an affront and a distraction to all the girls and Nora would pay for it. A tear formed in Valeria's eyes as she thought of her old friend. How she hoped that she had escaped, that she had found a way out of the orphanage and the cruelty of Miss June.

She let out a sigh, there was nothing she could do. Maybe she would try again soon. But this time she would sneak out and just hide around the corner. If she were lucky she would see Nora coming out for water or one of the other girls she trusted. If she could get a note to her friend it would be something.

Thinking back to the books, many of which were far beyond her ability to read, she found the idea of being surrounded by the stories of thousands of Nora's from all places and times comforting to her whether she could read them all or not.

Miss Umbridge had her read from the romances of Walter Scott and Edmund Spenser most evenings.

The old lady would help her a little with the long or odd words which Valeria couldn't always sound out. The books suggested a whole other way of living other than that of the heaped-up higgledy-piggledy of London's sprawling boroughs.

She had learned a great deal in her time working for Miss Umbridge who, despite a stern aspect had been kind to her. Treating her more as a companion than just as a maid. While Valeria did light housework, her duties tended to lean more towards companionship and helping Miss Umbridge with her daily toilette and keeping her company.

Valeria rocked up onto her tiptoes to move the next few books out of the way when the over-sprung bolt of the library door banged loudly as the handle turned and the door swung open.

The gentleman who swept in was talking charmingly with the cook as if they were old friends and there was no difference of class between them. Cook was clearly enjoying such attentions, for the gentleman was really quite handsome, and was talking back in a way that struck Valeria as outright impertinent.

Raising a hand to her mouth she tried to stifle a

laugh, but both gentleman and cook heard her efforts and turned to face her.

"Good morning, Sir," Valeria said and curtseyed.

He made half the shape of a greeting of his own with his mouth before cook jumped in.

"Dear me, Valeria — that is, Miss Collins, here — I had quite forgot you was cleaning the library — If I'd known I'd have had you wait in the drawing room, Mr Wright, Sir"

"Not a problem, Cookie. I shall be most careful not to disturb Miss Collins' work."

He turned and gave her a shallow bow, and as he straightened up his eyes moved slowly from Valeria's feet, up her black uniform and lingered over the white apron which covered her breast. Then he gave a quick dismissive flick up over neck, head and bonnet and his appraisal was complete. On his face was a warm smile, which suggested familiarity without condescension. Turning back to Cook he bid her take his calling card up to the mistress of the house.

Valeria was familiar with Mister Wright as part of the

cast of characters that made up the gossip of the house. He was Miss Umbridge's lawyer, of great talent and with a decent fortune. It was said that he was from no better a class of person than any of the staff.

The role of Miss Umbridge's lawyer made him a regular visitor since he was a kind of caretaker of her varied financial and real estate holdings. This was the first time Valeria had seen more than a glimpse of him moving down a corridor or passing through a doorway though and she decided she did not feel entirely comfortable in his presence.

"Please, do not allow me to hold you up, Miss Collins." His eyes seemed to bore into hers in a way that made it hard to return to work.

When she didn't immediately turn back to her dusting he took a step towards her. "Have you been with Miss Umbridge long?" he asked.

There was a sincerity in the question that drew Valeria in, she felt close to confiding in him when his eyes once more traced the outline of her figure, and she caught something shark-like in his smile.

"Almost two years, Sir."

"It is a wonder we have not yet crossed paths for I am in and out of this house like Miss Umbridge's personal jack-in-the-box."

He continued to study her without shame.

Valeria knew that her cheeks were flash hot and that she was blushing. The last two years of decent meals, warm beds, and kindness had allowed her to put on some weight leaving behind the sexless rail thin shape which every girl in the orphanage had retained well into puberty. She was never more aware of the womanhood in her figure than under the crawling gaze of this Mister Wright.

"As I say, I... I have been here almost... almost two years now, Sir. Miss Umbridge has been most kind to me in that time."

"She is a marvellous old bird, isn't she?"

He was studying her face now, although she felt no less like one of the insects in a book on etymology. Pinned and viewed under a glass, she felt less of the creeping shame she felt when he cast his eye over the apron string which cinched her waist.

"I wouldn't dare put it quite so boldly, Sir. But she is a fine woman, and a kind mistress."

"Yes," he said as if coming to a realisation. "You are quite right. Kind. That is the word for her. A very Christian lady."

He was standing quite close to Valeria now and she had to look up to meet his eye. She felt a chill in her gut and recognised it as fear but didn't understand quite why. He was being friendly, charming even...

The bolt shot again with its over-sprung violence and Valeria started dropping her rag and putting her hand to her mouth to stifle a small shout. Cook bustled back into the room holding the door for Miss Umbridge.

"Thomas, my dear boy, welcome. I hope Cook here has offered you something to drink."

His attention passed from Valeria like a cloud from the face of the sun. Spinning around he made sure all his charm fell on Miss Umbridge.

Valeria breathed again and bent to pick up the dust cloth.

"Cook, Valeria, my dear, would you two leave Mister

Wright and me to discuss some private matters please. You can finish dusting later. I am sure I shall not look at those tedious books before I die anyway. Start with the fiction section next time."

"Of course, Miss." Valeria curtseyed and walked — though she had a sudden urge to run — to the door.

Miss Umbridge was already talking about seeing to some private papers she was holding in her desk and the need for a better place to keep them.

"It's not secure enough, Mister Wright, but I hate not to have something on hand in case of emergencies."

As Valeria closed the door behind her, she cast an eye of her own over Mister Wright, he was looking right at her once more, only his eyes did not meet hers. They were focused lower down.

Valeria shivered as she pulled the door closed and the stiff spring of the lock slammed out another hefty bang.

CHAPTER THREE

*T*he pavement sent jolting pain up Allen's shins with every step. What with dodging the piles of horse leavings and avoiding putting his ankle out wherever one of the cobbles was missing he had almost forgotten his pursuers. Then he heard the cut glass shout of the gentleman and the lower cockney twang of his two servants.

They had been shouting, "Stop, thief," in increasingly out of breath tones for the full length of Grope Lane. Now they had followed him into this rather seedy back road despite the signs of dissolute living that surrounded them.

Allen was angry with himself. It had been a stupid

mistake to make, going for the pocket watch when he already had the man's wallet away clean. It wasn't greed that made him try the pin that linked the watch-chain to the man's waistcoat, but the thrill. Somewhere out there men were cutting their way into jungles, or scaling mountains for the same reason. Whatever the reason he had made the lapse and it had been stupid. Utterly stupid.

Allen swerved into an alley that he knew led behind a bakers with a faulty window latch. With luck he might squeeze through and get out of sight. As he turned he glanced behind him at the gentleman. The man looked in some disarray with his fat red face almost purple from shouting and running. He was little danger, but his cockney servants, despite their ridiculous livery, were dealing with the roads as well as Allen. They looked fit and were better fed than him. The men were keeping pace and maybe even closing in a little.

Not at his fittest, Allen was heaving up his own lungs. A bout of colic a few weeks ago had weakened him and he could feel a retching, phlegmatic cough building. It was also stupid to go out cutting purses and picking pockets when he wasn't right in body and mind. Thieving took focus. He should have stuck with the shoe shine job a little longer. The pay was awful and the work left his back out of shape and his polishing arm hurting so badly it could hardly move. Still, no one was gonna lock him up or hang him for blacking a boot wrong. A kick maybe, that happened several times a day. More than one fella had failed to pay up for work done, but a kick was a warm bath compared to the courthouse.

Allen ran as hard as he could rounding the corner in a slide, before the fellows on his tail could get eyes on him, he flung the watch and wallet into a particularly vile looking midden heap. Saying a silent prayer that they would be dung proof enough to keep their valuable innards safe from the heap of manure. They went straight down to disappear from view and with the incriminating evidence dispatched, he felt a bit lighter.

Perhaps too light, throwing the wallet knocked him off balance and a slight misstep had his shoe catch on a cracked paving slab. Arms wheeling, he went down hard, feeling his teeth crack together. His knees were skinned,and stung horribly and for a moment the world went a little funny at the edges.

But his fall gave him a new perspective on the street, someone had parked a handcart with a cracked spoke up against the wall. The cart was packed with large clay jars, but the straw they were packed in hung over the sides in thick curtains. Quickly, he rolled over and slipped under the cart just as the three men rounded the corner.

Holding his breath he watched as they sprinted past, and disappeared around the corner behind the bakery. The sound of their feet could be heard at the far end of the street, their shouts becoming less convinced the further they ran.

Safe, he climbed out from under the cart in an instant. A quick rummage in the midden heap returned the watch and wallet to his pocket. Soaked and stinking he set off in the opposite direction and a few minutes later he was in the clear. Strolling out towards the East End and attracting the odd curled lip and wrinkled nose from other pedestrians. He couldn't help but smile. Who cared what he smelt like when he had three full pound-notes in his pocket along with a fistful of copper coins and a few silver shillings.

It was a prince's haul, a year's room and board if the landlady or landlord didn't run him into the police the minute they saw a waif and stray like him with genuine banknotes in hand.

The day felt lighter but he was no fool and kept his eyes peeled as he walked. A strange sensation set in his stomach and he was sure, at least three times, that he saw a man following him. Each time he reminded himself that he was hardly worth following. But the man had a distinctive face, gaunt and long and was definitely moving in the same direction.

Taking a detour he ducked down a narrow and rubbish strewn lane. It would get him down near the Thames, and would hopefully shake off the imagined tail he had acquired. When he reached the river he could watch the ships and spend one of his coppers. His stomach rumbled at the thought. A whole baked potato and a bowl of soup from an old man hunched over a handcart full of hot coals.

Allen warmed himself as he ate and spoke to the old man who had lost a leg fighting the French, though he could not remember if it had been the Empire or the Republic. Allen listened intently to the man's rambling stories of forced marches and derring-do, then with a stomach heavy with food for the first time in two days he headed onwards to see what he could do about holing up for the night.

He turned away from the old sewage stink of Father Thames and into the fresher sewage stink of the East End. Taking a few alleys in the rough direction he soon passed into the familiar network of smog blackened buildings. They were built so close over the roads that their eaves seemed to blot out the sky.

Valeria's orphanage was around here somewhere, a nightmare prison run by that old harridan, Miss June. How he missed Valeria and how he hoped she was safe. Those nights they would sit and talk outside, so long ago, he had seen what his life might have been like after his mother passed.

He still dreamed of his mother some nights, coughing up blood and begging him to pray over her. He could never tell if the images came from memory, or if he had created them himself. Sometimes he dreamed of Valeria too. Those dreams were nicer but she was better off without him. Who wanted to know a gutter rat, a pickpocket, a thief?

His thoughts on dreams carried him right up to the wreck of the old brewery. The building had burned down. By some miracle the fire seemed to have done little but char the neighbouring houses and so the brewery stood like a rotted molar in the even jaw of the street. Looking both ways and seeing no one he scrambled through the window and off the street. Ducking under the charcoalised beams of what had been the ceiling he found the cellar door and listened for a bit.

Nothing but rats moving below.

Excellent, he thought and, careful to avoid the weak third step, he descended into the dark.

His eyes did not adjust immediately so he heard them before he saw stars. The rustle of cloth and the whisper of breath, then they were standing over him jeering and he was trying to shake his head clear of the agonising pain that rushed through it.

"If it isn't little Allen," said a voice he immediately recognised. It came from the silhouette, shadow on shadow, of Michael Potter. He was a year or so younger than Allen, but a good six inches taller and was followed about by a little crowd of waif's he'd rescued from orphanages or chimney sweeping.

Allen knew for a fact there was at least one boy dead at Michael's hands, so he lay pretty still and said in what he hoped was a friendly voice, "Ahoy, Michael. A little rougher than usual in your greeting. If I sit up, you gonna clout me again."

Allen's eyes were adjusting a little to the dark now. He could make out at least three other figures in the gloom.

"I'd stay down for the moment, little Allen. It's dark in here and it would be a sad thing if I were to stick you on my marlinspike."

Something metal glinted a little in the darkness. It looked longer and nastier than a marlinspike. Allen stayed down. He was sure he felt a rat scurry over his hand.

"I don't see I'm much to scare you and yours," Allen said. "I'm sorry if I disturbed you. I didn't realise the brewery was taken for the night. I guess it's best I sod off and leave you and yours in peace, eh?"

Micheal leaned in, the little light from the cellar door

was beginning to pervade the room and Allen could see his humourless smile clearly. "No, Allen. I think you should stay. Maybe share some of your takings today. Think of it as rent. You got some bread on you."

Allen felt his heart sink. If they found his haul, that was a fee worth killing for. He looked again at the knife in Michael's hand and with a quick flick of his foot kicked it free of his grip. The knife skittered away into the dark.

Before Michael could react, Allen slammed a fist into his nose and made for the stairs. Heart pounding, arms swinging he was halfway there, but one of the other shadows got in his way and brought him to the floor with a fist to the solar plexus.

The next few minutes were a welter of pain. It became immediately apparent that Michael couldn't find his knife because Allen remained un-stabbed for the full extent of the kicking he received.

To protect himself he lay with hands over his face, curled up into a ball. After a while the blows stopped and hands rummaged through his pockets. He stayed stock still, in a ring circumscribed by the edges of his pain. He heard the voices vanish, and he lay like that for what seemed like hours. Too hurt to move but it was a mental hurt as well as a physical one. All that work, all that money, the food it represented, the warmth, the possibility of shoes and a coat, all of it evaporated, borne off by the laughter of Michael and his gang.

Allen lay there until he slept.

He woke to find himself warmed from in front by a small fire and from behind by the bruises that he could feel covering his back. In front of him a pile of small wooden parts of the brewery glowed hot with a small tin cup resting in the embers.

On the other side of the fire a gaunt looking man was sat, his large nose casting a moving shadow on the rest of his face as he stoked the fire up.

"Hey now, young man. You look like you took a substantial beating. I assume it wasn't those fellas you robbed what done you in this way?"

"Who the blazes are you?" Allen snapped.

"Of course, my name's Taylor — Mr Abel Taylor. Would you care for something to eat?"

Allen sat up straight and gave the man a close look. "You *were* following me."

"No, I was trying to catch up to you. I lost you for a bit after you shook that toff, but I have a hound dog's instinct for these things. I see you are rather better at acquiring than retaining."

"What?"

"I checked your pockets for the loot, and it was quite gone. Just this copper in the folds of your shirt." The coin flashed in Mr Abel Taylor's hand for a moment. "You may have it back if you like, but I would recommend you offer it to me by way of an agenting fee."

Taylor's mouth curled into a smirk.

"I'll take my coin, please."

"Eat first." Taylor leaned forward with a heel of bread in one hand and passed the mug from the fire to Allen with the other.

Allen took both and dipped the bread into the warm savoury broth. He swallowed a mouthful. "Thank you, Mr Taylor, Sir..."

"Please, boy, Taylor to you and anyone else under God's sky. I don't believe in rank or age. I am a man of capital." He flicked the coin up in the air and caught it with his other hand as it came down. "For your capital, I will make a great return."

"What do you mean a return?"

"A job, boy — Might I know your name?"

Allen told him.

"A job, Allen. And more importantly for a man who sleeps in a cellar, room and board while you work for me."

"A job, you say?" Allen asked. He looked Taylor up and down, he didn't like it, but anything to get off the street, he thought.

"Aye, fair pay for hard work and a place to rest your weary bones."

"What kind of work?"

"The sort you've been doing all your life, my boy, but with far greater ambition."

"It sounds better than the streets."

Taylor spat in his hand and offered it to him. Allen followed suit and they shook. "I guess you're my man now, Allen."

"I guess so, Taylor."

The feeling of signing a deal with the devil didn't leave Allen until he was back at Taylor's house and curled up on the straw in his own bed.

CHAPTER FOUR

*N*ora stood beneath the black doors to William Richmond's house, just off Baker Street, and nearly an hour's walk from the orphanage — Miss June would not pay for transport. The imposing three-story building was set back from the road with a small patch of greyish green grass attempting to grow in front of it and the faint glow of morning lamplight showing at the edges of the curtains.

It had been two days since she had fainted at the sewing table. Miss June had quarantined her for twenty-four hours in a small cupboard to keep her from infecting the other girls. However, it had soon become clear that Nora's ailment, if any, was not catching. So she had been hauled back out into the light and along with Sophie and a few of the other more responsible girls, had been told that Miss June had found them some rather better use for their time.

She was given one of the dresses in better repair and a small slip of paper. On it was written an address she was unable to read. Now she wished she had learned to read like Valeria had. It was too late, she was sent out a full hour before dawn to find her way to this residence to which she had been, as Miss June put it, "rented out".

Asking directions she arrived at the house. It looked pleasant but nothing too grand. She lifted the knocker and let it fall three times against the front door — there was no servant's entrance that she could make out. From within the house, beyond the door, she could make out the heartbeat sounds of someone coming down a flight of stairs. A few moments later the door was opened by the meanest, dourest man Nora had ever seen. He frowned down at her with his eyebrows wrinkled into a furious glare.

"You are Miss June's girl?" he asked with an imperious voice.

Nora curtseyed and lowered her eyes taking in the man's livery and cheap but perfectly polished shoes. "Yes, Sir."

"Please," he said in a voice that still seemed to convey utter contempt. "Call me Stephen. I am head of Mr. Richmond's household staff. You are on time which is a fact I greatly value, even if the master does not. Name, girl?"

"Nora."

"Welcome, Nora. Have you breakfasted?"

"I have," Nora lied, hoping to keep Stephen happy. One look at his face suggested that might be a difficult task.

Stephen led Nora into the house, through a meticulously tidy front hall, past brass and two mirrors, polished to perfection. Each of the mirrors showed a reflection of the other ad infinitum.

Taken into a smaller room she was given a uniform, ironed wool dress, starched cotton apron, white hat.

All perfectly creased and spotlessly clean. She dressed in the small servants quarters, then headed back into the hall.

From the hall she was led into a tightly turning stairwell. The wood was polished so smooth she worried the nails in her shoes might scratch it. Even the stair railings shone with a terrifying degree of cleanliness.

As they reached the top of the stairs Nora could hear all manner of animal sounds, birds tweeting, flies buzzing, the scratches of small rodents and the barking of a dog. She noted that the upstairs landing showed no signs of these animals. Not a stray hair or feather in sight.

There were four doors on the landing. Each one tall, dark wood, and like everything else in the house, shining like brand new.

"As you have eaten, you best get to work directly. While I am proud to serve my, and now your, master outside these four doors, we have come to an agreement that he shall hire additional help to assist in keeping order behind them. You will take your orders from him directly, come to me should you need any point of procedure explaining. I am more than willing to assist in helping you in whatever way I can. Yours is a Herculean task most reminiscent of the Stygian Horses."

Nora smiled, for she knew the story of these flesh-eating horses whose stables had to be cleaned by Hercules in one day. He did it by diverting a river through their filthy stables. She looked around at the extraordinary spotlessness and couldn't understand how this related. The master was clearly a stickler.

Stephen put a hand on her shoulder. His voice never wavered from his condescending tone, and no smile showed in his eyes or lips, but the gesture suggested kindness beneath the carefully manicured façade. "If you need anything..." he said.

He cocked his ear and, based on the strange noises, selected one of the four doors. He opened it and ushered Nora through.

Now she understood. The room was a mess. No animal sounds emanated from within, apart from the loud snoring of the Staffordshire terrier which was curled up by the fire. It looked so cute but she was a little afraid. Dogs were often hungry and had been known to steal your food.

The room was in total disarray. Along two walls were long benches carrying a vast array of glass beakers, copper burners, steel racks and stands. These were piled like dirty dishes at one end. A more ordered collection appeared to be in the process of distilling something tar black in a large glass bulb among the detritus on one of the tables. The other was set up for some experiment Nora couldn't even begin to fathom.

Upon one wall were overfull bookshelves, against which leaned stacks of more books. Many were open and showing extensive marginal notes in a scruffy hand. The other wall was covered in disordered shelves of jars, bottles and spare chemical equipment. At the window, the Master stood in a filthy apron encrusted with the dying effects of compounds of every colour.

Nora felt a little overwhelmed but her eyes kept on roaming.

On the table were piles of paper, two microscopes

and an array of potted plants turning varying degrees of brown. It was chaotic.

Stephen appeared hardly able to look at the mess and stared intently at his master's face. "Your new maid, Sir," he announced. Then, he bowed and left the room hurriedly doing his best not to look directly at the appalling mess.

Mister William Richmond gave Nora a quick glance up and down with his deep brown eyes. He had long, rather effeminate lashes which softened his sharp features, with their high cheekbones and slightly pointed nose. He looked like he had been machine tooled. His black hair was long but swept back perfectly neatly and in his gloved hands he held a clay jar from which billowed an acrid smoke.

"Hello, Miss," he said, flashing her a smile of perfect, white teeth. "I'm sure Stephen has entirely failed to tell you your duties, or in fact to prepare you in any way. He does get terribly upset about how I keep these rooms, so he stays in the main house and does a fantastic job of keeping the whole place shipshape. The labs require you though."

"Of course, Sir."

"Anything living, you're better off not touching at first, lest they bite, sting, or squirt foul-smelling liquids on you. I'll also need to show you how to clean some of the more sensitive materials. And in here, if it it is solid, liquid or gas, you're best not touching it at all unless I tell you too. Some of this stuff is rather potent and others could put a whole nunnery to sleep for good." He stopped and gave a little chuckle.

"You will get used to the labs, but for now, the bedroom is the main thing you can easily get into order. Keep the bed clear for me to sleep in, and ensure I have a clean set of clothes for the following morning. Two sets in fact. One set of something natty in case I go out and some work clothes in case I decide to stay in and work on my projects. If I were you I'd put more care into the latter set as I am rather more likely to make use of those. Apart from those tasks the job is really just odds and ends as and when I need you, and keeping the labs tidy. I would hardly have bothered hiring someone if Stephen weren't so insistent. It looks a mess but really everything is in something like its proper place. Except that... and that... and..." He cast his gaze about the room. "Well, I think you get the sense of it, no?"

"Yes, Sir."

"Well, you're clearly a lass of few words. We can do the getting to know you stuff in a bit; for now, if you try that door to the left, that will take you to my sleeping quarters. Just run a duster over everything and take the washing down to Stephen and I'll give you a shout if I need anything."

He smiled again, and her stomach seemed to flutter a little. He seemed kind, just a change from Miss June, even the dour old Stephen was clearly soft under his tyrannical need for tidiness. There was also the fact that Mister Richmond was terribly good looking. She smiled back and went to try the door.

It was locked.

"Ah, sorry there, lass," Mister Richmond said. He started pulling out drawers under the desk and rummaging through what looked like the mix of discards from a farriers yard and the reading room of the British Library.

Eventually, he let out a cry of triumph and produced a ring of old brass keys. "Here we are."

He passed the keys to Nora, cold metal and warm

flesh touched her hand as he pressed the right key down.

"Thank you, Sir." She curtseyed again awkwardly.

"I wouldn't worry too much about formality here; so long as you don't get in the way and keep up with the work I'm not a difficult man to please." He smiled at her again, then his gaze turned back to the smoking clay jar.

Nora set to work in the bedroom. It turned out that while the main tasks of stripping and changing the bed, putting the clothes out to be washed by Stephen and making sure that there were two sets of clothes for the morning took no time at all, Nora's work was constantly interrupted by the *brief* demands of Mister Richmond's work.

"Nora, could you clean up those beakers there for me, use the scourers in the sink."

She rushed about from job to job, watching the list of things to do get longer.

"When you're done with those could you fetch another thermometer from the other lab."

Occasionally, the instructions featured some obscure word she had no hope of understanding.

"I need the galvanometer and the larger of the three lodestones in the horology cabinet." By the time she got back to the beakers she was so flustered she dropped one, smashing it.

Freezing to the spot fear raised the hairs on her arms. *Lord, no*, she thought, panicking. *I'm in for it now.*

Miss June would have taken a meal away or had Sophie whip her with a birch twig. Instead, she heard Mister Richmond chuckle.

"Careful there, lass. Take it slow, use those leather gloves, and don't worry."

It seemed he understood her panic and perplexity.Turning to look at her with a kindly smile. "There is a great deal in these rooms that mean nothing to men just as educated as me, just as in the labs of other scientists there are a myriad of things that are total mysteries to me. One can't know everything about everything. One specialises. You are beginning to specialise in the workings of these labs of mine. Ask as many questions as you need. It will bring you up to speed all the faster."

Nora wasn't sure what to say. "Thank you, Sir." She curtseyed, but he had already turned back to his work.

Letting out a breath her shoulders relaxed as she realised she was in no trouble.

As she pulled on the gloves and removed the shards of glass from the sink, he carried on speaking to her about his experiment. He used a great many new words like "hydrocarbon" and "precipitation" and others she recognised but were combined in ways that made little sense "chemical bond" and "electrical charge". As far as she could make out he wanted to separate two liquids mixed together and his current method wasn't working.

"I shall have to write all this up."

"But, Sir. If it hasn't worked what is there to write up? What can you learn from a lesson that failed?" she asked.

"You have learned that it doesn't work, of course. In science a negative result is still a positive fact. Less exciting perhaps than learning the right answer. But knowing that one theory is wrong gets you a little closer to one that is right."

"I see, Sir," she said, going back to scrubbing the glassware clean. It had a strange smell when the water touched it, and she found her head hurt from the fumes.

"Could you stop for a moment, I want to show you how this still works so that you can keep an eye on it for me during tomorrow's work session."

Nora nodded feeling strangely happy to be included in his work.

Her first day ended late, sending her hurrying back to the orphanage in the dark. Mister Richmond had Stephen give her some cold meat to eat when she got home and she hungrily devoured it en route knowing that Miss June would only take it for herself if she still had it when she got back.

It proved fortuitous for Miss June sent her straight up to her pallet with the other girls without food.

"If you wanted to eat you shouldn't have dawdled on the way home," she snapped.

DESPITE MISS JUNE'S IRE, Nora slept well. Even Sophie digging her elbows into her back didn't bother her. She had worked hard, felt kindness and eaten well. She might as well have been in heaven.

The next few days were much the same. She learned to feed the two monkeys who were being studied for signs of human-like emotions. The fruit flies that were being crossbred to determine aspects of heredity that may shed light on Messrs Darwin and Wallace's ideas of 'descent with modification'. He also taught her how to tend to the many different plants that grew under the bay windows in a little indoor glasshouses.

She learned to clean the telescopes which Mister Richmond claimed were *bloody useless* since the introduction of gaslight on every through fare in London.

"We've blotted out the stars, even the moon looks hazy through the smog," he moaned with that strange smile that always lit up his face. The man loved his work.

She also learned how to look after the delicate moving parts of his microscopes which he said were a far better use of the lens for a city gent like himself.

It seemed that Mister Richmond cared for almost

nothing else in the world but finding out new things. Striding around his lab he asked relentlessly of himself, "What is the reason?" Then, he set about hunting for an answer.

If it was not in his books, he wrote letters asking others. "What is the reason for this?" If they came back without an explanation he set to interrogating nature with his instruments to find out the reason for himself.

Working with him was exciting and interesting. There was so much to learn and he was never cruel. She was always warm and well cared for and every day she was fed at least one meal that was worth more than a weeks worth of food from the orphanage.

One day he showed her his paper and read it out to her. He had published one of the first monographs on the underlying musculature of bees and showed Nora the incredibly detailed etchings he had made and the pencil originals.

She was astonished by the breadth of his talents, and when she suggested as much he looked rather sad.

"I had a very hard father," he replied. "He drove me

to excellence in all things. I rather think I haven't taken a moment off from study since I was old enough to learn my alphabets. You can acquire a great deal of knowledge if you keep looking, keep asking questions. "

While they worked he explained, as best he could, in the most haphazard way all the new science of the age. Nora tried to understand, though without knowing the underpinnings of it all, it may as well have been necromancy to her. But it clearly helped him to think when he talked through his work with her and so she listened intently and asked questions whenever it seemed like it might help him to unravel his own thoughts.

The rest of the time was scut-work. Cleaning, dusting, picking up after the incorrigible sloven, for a disinterest in the world outside of his passionate search for the secrets of nature had led him to ask, "What is the reason for tidiness?" It seemed he had found there to be no positive answer.

Books were left wherever he last consulted them. Often atop other books, or dangerous chemicals. Nora would often pause to look upon these books; he had taught her a very few words. These however were well beyond her abilities and she could hardly pick out more than a few words on each page.

Almost every possible surface within the lab was hung with a dirty apron. Nora would take these out to Stephen, to be washed. It seemed excessive at first but he explained that he changed his lab clothes frequently to prevent contamination between tests.

Through all this Nora was to do her best to keep in check and perhaps even work against the tide of disarray that he lived in. Slowly returning books to the shelves in a new system she worked out as she went along. She spent nearly every minute of the working day in his presence. Talking to him first in reverent tones, then in conversation. Soon she felt comfortable with him in a way she hadn't felt with anyone since Valeria.

Gradually, he became someone who might not just be her elder, better, and employer, but something more like a friend. To her joy she knew that he felt of her in the same way. Their conversations were interesting to both of them and her care was helping him care better for himself.

At night she would walk back to the orphanage and

sink under the cold blankets and feel happy because the next day she would walk out the doors again. She would return to warmth and light and the scowling face of kind old Stephen and the lopsided but charming smile of Mister Richmond.

She woke every morning now without fear.

CHAPTER FIVE

*V*aleria's room in Miss Umbridge's house was a source of daily joy for her. She had a few hours to herself after finishing her housework early, and before Cook would need a hand in the kitchen. She was using the time to read, as she usually did.

The book in her hand was the first volume of Chapman's *Odyssey*, it made her dizzy to read a book that was printed over one hundred years ago. To think that it was a two hundred and fifty-year-old translation of the words of a man who first told the story in Ancient Greek made her feel so wonderful. She could read the book, telling a story some thousand years before Christ was born. The sense of time made her feel woozy, like she was in touch with not just a ghost but perhaps one of heaven's messengers.

The book lay open on her lap, the leaves open like wings, and it told her the story of the man who — as she read aloud to herself.

"Wound with his wisdom to his wished stay, that wandered wondrous far, when he the town of sacred Troy had sack'd and shivered down. The cities of a world of nations, with all their manners, minds, and fashions, he saw and knew; at sea felt many woes, Much care sus... sus t..a...i...ned... sustained." Occasionally she had to stop and sound out the words. It didn't matter, the story intrigued her so she read on. "...sustained to save from overthrows Himself and friends in their retreat for home; but so their fates he could not overcome, though much he thirsted it. O men unwise, They perish'd by their own impieties."

Miss Umbridge had read her these lines in the original Greek and explained each word slowly, making Valeria write them down over and over again in the foreign script. Miss Umbridge was teaching her many things. Though she would pretend to be indifferent to the knowledge in her library, Miss Umbridge knew a great deal and enjoyed sharing her knowledge. Valeria was delighted to share, to read, to converse and to listen to her employer talking.

As well as having Valeria read to her most afternoons from adventure novels and romances like *Robinson Crusoe, Don Quixote,* and *Evelina,* Miss Umbridge would also talk to her about art, science, politics and religion. Sometimes she would send Valeria away to read a passage from some poem or to consult some engraving of a great painting in one of the many catalogues that lined the library's shelves. She would always begin by asking Valeria what she thought.

"I miss real conversation," Miss Umbridge would say. "I want to hear your mind on this subject."

It made Valeria feel foolish to opine about an image of Michelangelo's paintings — which Miss Umbridge said had been censored by whoever made the engravings.

"The men have all their wedding tackle out in every one of these paintings and statues. When it comes to Michelangelo, you can hardly move for the forest of phalluses. It is most disappointing to see the British public cannot be expected to view such things as beautiful without also being sordid about it."

Valeria had blushed at such a conversation and pretended that she was sitting a little close to the fire. It had became clear very quickly to Valeria that Miss Umbridge was a powerful intellect. One who, in a man's body would have been pursuing science or mastering industry. It left her sad, that such a woman had been so contained by her sense of what society would tolerate from her that it left her unfulfilled.

Even with Valeria she would often pretend to be uninterested or ignorant of a subject she had been waxing lyrical and loquaciously on just the day before. These were both words that Valeria enjoyed greatly once Miss Umbridge had explained them to her after she had struggled through them in a volume of Scott, just the day before.

The current book in her hands was difficult. The words were in a strange order and the old spellings were sometimes impossible to follow. That line she recognised though, the Biblical account of tragedy: "Oh men unwise, They perish'd by their own impieties."

Line by line she unfolded the story of Odysseus who had left home for greater things and abandoned his wife, "wise Penelope", and son, "God-like Telemachus", to the ravages of "thee shameless suitors".

The opening books about Telemachus' trials in his father's absence seemed to pierce Valeria's heart. She had left people behind just as Odysseus had. Nora, in Miss June's horrible orphanage, and Allen, lost out there on the streets, suffering God knows what. But unlike Odysseus, Valeria was not making her way back, to reunite them in a moment of homecoming. She was stuck here, unwilling or unable to leave Calypso's isle.

A tear blurred out some line of Pallas Athena's and she put the book aside for fear of getting the pages wet.

What had happened to Nora? she wondered, doing her best to imagine a perfect outcome for her friend. Adoption into a kind family, marriage to an eligible young man, maybe a small child for Nora to tell her stories to.

Her reveries were blotted out by the panicked face of Cook poking her head around her door.

"Oh Lord, Miss Valeria. That bloody dog has gone and done it." Cook's face was bright red. "I chased the little bugger down, but it was too late. You'll have to go into town and pick up another."

"Another what, Cookie?"

"A duck, Miss Valeria. The dog stole this evening's duck. I only got the one and we have a ham but Miss Umbridge was terribly insistent that it be duck this evening, as it is Mister Wright's favourite and, oh Lord, my kingdom for a duck, Ducky."

"Oh dear, Cookie. I'll go right away."

To be honest with herself, she was a little pleased at the errand. She wanted to get out of the house. Her books were a delight, and to have so many, was such a great privilege, but she worried she was getting too much inside her own head of late and a walk to the market and back would be the perfect way to cheer herself up. The city was always especially alive at this time of day and she liked the man who Cookie insisted on getting poultry from. He had a disreputable air that reminded her of the rakes and cads in the books of Samuel Richardson.

THE MARKET WAS FAR BUSIER than usual when she arrived, and the poultry merchant had a queue before his stall. In the feather-speckled mud of the courtyard she stood and waited. Watching the sun lower in the sky. There was no doubt about it, dinner would be late. Poor Mister Wright would have to wait and talk more about bonds and shares and all the other secret papers of Miss Umbridge's desk.

Meanwhile, Valeria got to enjoy the smells and sounds of the market. The rich smell of animals alive and dead, their leavings and their feed. Across the way the walls of fruit and vegetables, carted in from the country, or brought in by barge or train, gave off their sweet smells and their bitter undercurrent of fermentation.

The stall owners shouted, advertising their wares.

"A bushel for six-pence."

"Pies, three for a shilling."

It all went over her head as the queue shortened a little and someone joined just behind her. A moment later she felt a movement. Like the wing of a bird against her dress. It took her a second to realise that the movement had lifted the weight of her purse and she turned. There was no one behind her in the queue anymore. Just off to the right, partially hidden by the crowd was a figure about her height. Slight and dressed rather poorly, though cleanly, his hand was slipping her purse into his own pocket.

She did not hesitate; hitching up her skirt she strode after him quickly, it appeared he thought he had got away clean and was not looking around for any pursuer. Perhaps he was just trying to look innocent should she have noticed. It would have worked too if she had taken just a moment longer to react.

Not wanting to spook him she walked quickly but calmly after him.

He disappeared into a small crowd and she broke into a little run to get around them. He was strolling out the far side and heading towards the queue for another stand. She reached him first and seized his wrist.

"I will take my purse back, Sir," she said. "Or I will raise the alarm and have you hung."

He turned around and her jaw dropped. So did his. For it was Allen.

They stood staring at each other for what felt like an age, in which time he seemed to glance about looking for somewhere to run, then half step forward as if to embrace her, then looked down as if ashamed. While these emotions played out on his face, Valeria felt only one: joy.

"My God, Allen. Where have you been all these years?"

"Valeria, I—" he took her purse out of his pocket and handed it to her. "I'm sorry, I didn't know it was you. I didn't recognise you. You've grown so much and your clothes... I guess you found someone to take you away from that awful place then?"

"Yes, I live in the most wonderful house as companion and maid to a truly fine lady. Oh, Allen. I cannot let you go now. We have so much to talk about."

He looked about quickly as if to check they were not being observed, then he smiled.

"Yes, let's catch up. We should go now though."

"Just one moment. I have to buy a duck for dinner. I do hope Cook doesn't mind my bringing you back. Miss Umbridge will insist on hosting you, she is terribly eccentric."

Allen looked a little uncomfortable at this delay, but dutifully joined her in the queue.

Valeria's head was rushing, her heart leaping. A great weight lifted for Allen, lovely Allen was okay and back in her life. She smiled and stood close to him in the queue, feeling the warmth of his body, so solid and real, so much more than any of the books or stories she had read in all that time at Miss Umbridge's.

"Men perish by their own impieties," she said to herself. "And women perish by the impieties of men."

CHAPTER SIX

"*T*hank you, Nora." Mr Richmond took the proffered cup of black tea, in which a bright yellow rind of a lemon floated. Nora had her own cup of tea, with almost more milk than tea in it. It was such a luxury for her to have a tea and milk. So much of a treat.

This had become a custom in the last few weeks, twice a day at eleven and four Nora would stop her bustling, and Mr Richmond would stop his inquiring into Nature. Then the two of them would drink tea in William's optics laboratory. It was not only the tidiest but the one in which there were no foul smells to ruin the tea and conversation.

"I swear Stephen's face is getting angrier," said

William, smiling lightly. "Have you left one of the teacups with the handle pointed a degree awry of the ceramic meridian?"

Nora chuckled. "You must be nicer about Stephen, Sir. His frown is like when I reattached the barometer to the thermometer." She raised her eyebrows at him and felt such joy that she didn't want there to be dissent between them. "The dial does not reflect the internal workings. He is a kind... and dare I say... a rather happy man, behind his furious face."

William laughed out loud and it made him look so carefree. "Perhaps you are right, but I do wish he'd smile at me. It reminds me terribly of how my father used to listen to me whenever he asked to what use I had put my day. I would excitedly tell him all about some mathematical formula my tutor had taught me and he would sit there like a rock, glowering. In his case though, I believe he truly hated me."

Nora gasped, the thought of having a parent was such a dream for her and to find that Stephen's had been so mean, it was a little disappointing.

"The difference is that Stephen really does care

about you, Mister Richmond. Not, perhaps, as much as he cares about keeping the house tidy." Once more she found herself smiling. "Do you never entertain?

"I do from time to time, but as most of my acquaintances are in London's scientific community it is far easier to meet them at the Athenaeum or the Royal Society. And it keeps Stephen from losing his mind cleaning up after the rowdiest drunks in London. If you've ever seen Hogarth's etchings on the gin craze you still have no real sense of the kind of debauches great mind's think up when they descend into booze. There is an awful lot of free thinking in the sciences."

"Oh, surely—" Nora was cut off by Stephen opening the door.

"A guest has arrived for you, Sir. A lady."

"Bring her up, we're not at work right now, Stephen."

Stephen turned around and left them. Returning a few moments later to find them still laughing at his expense. Nora felt rather bad for him, when he had been so kind, but Mr Richmond did such a funny impression of Stephen she couldn't help it. Besides,

Stephen's good humour was evident despite the unfortunate arrangement of his features.

She was still laughing when Mr Richmond's guest arrived. Nora's heart froze and the smile died on her lips. Miss June stood in the doorway, her frown externally matched Stephen's precisely, but Nora knew the vast difference in sentiment that lay behind her expression.

"You are needed, Nora." Her eyes seemed to be fixed on Nora's mouth, where a moment ago a smile of real joy had played. Nora could feel that gaze reading her and boring into her. The cold of Miss June's expression seemed to fill her up, forcing out the warmth of Mister Richmond's charm and kindness.

Without a word Nora put down her cup and crossed the room. She turned and, unable to look him in the eye, or even speak, curtseyed and passed out the door with Miss June.

They walked wordlessly out the house, down the street, and only when they had passed from view of the house did Miss June turn to Nora and open her mouth.

"You little hussy," she snarled.

Nora could see in Miss June's face a burning hatred, an anger that must stretch back in time to some hurt in her past. The hatred was so deep it seemed to turn Miss June from a woman into a gargoyle. In slow motion Nora saw this monster raise its hand and, with open palm, slap Nora in the face.

The blow stung, but the real pain was the humiliation. Men walked back and forth in expensive suits, looking at her with pity and disgust, she saw Mister Richmond's face in all of them.

"You think you can whore yourself out do you? You'll not make a brothel of my institution," Miss June screamed the words spraying her with spittle.

"I...I didn't," Nora stuttered through the tears. She felt shame searing her cheeks and clogging up her throat and couldn't get the words out. It hurt that she couldn't defend herself, or William, from this attack.

"And you won't." Miss June's face was so red it looked as if she might explode. "You will never visit that place again. Never see that man again. And never leave the orphanage again."

Nora felt numb, the door to her greatest hope, so narrowly cracked open, had slammed shut in her face. In the time she had been working for William, she had dared to dream of happiness. It had grown inside her so recently, never really taking form. She did not know what she expected, what foolish dream she had imagined but she knew that in his house, in his company, she was truly happy. To never see William again, to never speak with Stephen, it was worse than never having met them for now she had tasted what life could be like. The two men were the only people, apart from Valeria, who had ever shown her... kindness... no... love. Though they would deny it their kind and compassionate treatment was more love than she knew how to cope with.

Just like Valeria, they too were now taken away from her, forever.

She wanted to cry, but no tears would come. She wanted to scream, to fight Miss June, to run back to the house off Baker Street and throw herself at Mister Richmond's mercy. Instead, she meekly nodded, and stared at Miss June's shoes.

Without another word Miss June stalked off down the street toward the orphanage. Nora followed her miserably, knowing that things would likely get worse. What would she suffer for this?

CHAPTER SEVEN

They walked into the entrance hall of the orphanage and Miss June turned on her once more. Nora had been rushed out of the house so fast, that she hadn't had the chance to change out of her uniform.

"Go to your room and take that off," Miss June let her eyes roll over the dress and apron. "I imagine selling it on might make up for some of the income you have cost me by your impertinence with Mister Wright.

Nora didn't understand what was happening, why Miss June was so furious, or what she had done wrong.

"I'm sorry," she said, again and again, feeling wretched and not understanding what she was saying it for. "It will never happen again."

"No, it will not. Get out of those clothes this instant, I will bring you your new uniform."

Head down, heart aching Nora walked up to the room where the girls clothes were left. Fighting back her tears she stripped down to her petticoat and reached for one of the dirty rags that was left in the room.

Miss June walked in and picked up the clean starched uniform. Nora picked up a thin grey cotton dress from the pile.

"Your petticoats too."

Nora bit back her tears and tried to swallow the lump in her throat. It wouldn't go down. Her hope was gone, her chance at a happy life. Slowly, she pulled the stiff and smelly dress on and shivered. It hardly kept the chill out at all. She went to put the shoes on that came with her job.

"No, you do not deserve shoes, those will be sold too. Come with me."

Miss June led Nora through to the dining hall where the girls sat at their tables still sewing away. Without a word to any of the other girls Miss June pulled her chair out to the front of the raised area where the food was normally served.

"Get up on that."

Nora moved to sit on it up in front of all the other girls, shame already coloured her cheeks.

"No, stand."

Nora clambered up, wobbling a little on the chair. Someone laughed, probably Sophie.

"This girl is an ungrateful brat and attempted to use my generous gift of employment to weasel her way into another's home, depriving me of my income and making me look like a brothel madam in the process. I want you all to look at her and understand that if you do not live right — by the laws of God and our Queen — you will end up like her."

Miss June picked up her Bible and began to read, "Then one of the seven angels who had the seven bowls came and talked with me, saying to me, 'Come, I will show you the judgment of the great harlot who sits on many waters, with whom the kings of the earth committed fornication, and the inhabitants of the earth were made drunk with the wine of her fornication…'"

Miss June read on, providing a concordance of all the passages of the Bible in which women were denigrated for their sins. Jezebel and Eve, Oholah and Oholibah, the lists of sin from Deuteronomy and Leviticus, and on and on.

The message, as Nora saw it, was far from subtle and wholly unjust. What had she done wrong?

Nora's legs began to ache. An hour passed. A cramp started up in the back of her calf. Her back ached. Then two hours passed. Miss June was working the girls much longer than usual and by the time they got their evening chores done they would be late to bed, precious hours of sleep stolen from them.

Nora knew they would blame her for all of it. Not Miss June's viciousness and volatile temper, her increasingly fanatical commitment to the protestant work ethic. With so obvious a scapegoat put before them, how could they fail to cast all their suffering back onto her.

Eventually Miss June closed the book and stood up.

"Before you go to your evening chores, each one of you will come to the front one by one and deliver a blow with this switch to Miss Pearson's person. Anyone who goes easy on her will be subject to a caning from me. Now form a line." She held a beating rod in her hand, a length of supple willow cut to sting.

Nora thought her heart might stop. Could this get any worse? As the girls sat, their eyes wide, Nora clenched her fists, hoping she would not cry out. For a moment she saw William's face, but the image would not stay, this was too much.

She had received canings before, all of them had. They had been as a punishment from Miss June for some sin that she could not remember. Those times she had received five, or ten strokes. This would be almost thirty blows.

"Up now, I gave you an order," Miss June barked.

There was a slow reluctant rising from the tables. Apart from in one spot where Sophie sprang up to her feet and ran to the front of the line.

"Your enthusiasm for justice does you credit, Sophie," Miss June said, handing her the willow switch. "Get down, child," she said to Nora.

With stiff limbs, Nora climbed down slowly and faced the woman who would *punish* her. Just a month ago her eyes would have been on the floor, but now she kept them on Miss June's even though she knew such insolence would cause her more harm.

With rough hands, Miss June turned Nora around and unlaced the back of her dress to expose her shoulders and back.

Nora breathed in sharply. The air was cold on her skin and she waited.

Sophie did not go easy.

The first blow cracked in a clean line across her shoulders filling Nora's world with pain. It stung like a line of needles right across her shoulder blades.

The next voice was that of Suzy, a young girl Nora had given special care to. She struck with much less force than Sophie. Nora's stomach went cold as Miss June said, "See me before bedtime, Suzy. That was no effort, no effort at all."

The next girl did not make the same mistake. Instead, she nearly broke the rod in her desire to stay on Miss June's good side. The blow knocked Nora to her knees. Miss June grabbed her by the wrist and pulled her back up to her feet.

"Stand and take your punishment, Nora. You cannot be forgiven if you do not repent."

"I'm sorry," she said again. It did no good.

The next girl had her turn, and Nora heard nothing from then on. Felt nothing beyond the thin strips of her back that stung with every blow. Nothing but the renewing of the pain, which faded to a stale throb between each blow, then was raised back to fresh agony with each new punishment. She didn't count them, nor did time mean much. At some point the burning in her back was no longer caused by new blows but by the rough hands of Miss June tying her dress back up. Was it over?

"I do not want you corrupting the other girls," Miss June said. "So you will speak to no one until I give you permission to again. You will sleep alone. You will eat alone. You will say your prayers alone."

She showed Nora to the quarantine room, a small

cupboard barely large enough to lie down in. Miss June pushed Nora inside with no blanket.

But at least no window to let in a draft, Nora thought. She tried to get comfortable, but every position hurt. Lying on her back set her bruises on fire, on her side her shoulders and hips pressed into the hardwood uncomfortably and on her front she found she breathed in the dust and cobwebs on the floor making her sneeze. When she sneezed it also set her bruises on fire.

Lying in the dark she felt the tears roll in hot rivulets across her face. She had felt so much happiness, so much hope in the last few weeks at Mister Richmond's house.

It seemed far crueler to have let her sample real friendship, real kindness and then snatch it away like this. Far crueler than simply leaving her to suffer with the other girls until she was old enough to be palmed off to the workhouse.

As she lay there she thought about all the times Mister Richmond had asked about the orphanage and how she had lied. Telling him that it was hard but fair, that life was tolerable and Miss June kind.

Looking back on it she could see he had been concerned, worried perhaps about exactly this sort of occurrence. She should have said something, perhaps he could have intervened, but no, that was foolish thinking. That silly treacherous hope still wanted to taunt her. No one was coming to rescue her. What else was there to do but lie down and take it. Could there be another way?

Sleep came upon her fitfully.

CHAPTER EIGHT

*N*ora woke in the night to the feel of a rat crawling over her bare feet. There was no revulsion, a rat was part of their everyday life. Clenching her fists and hugging her arms around herself she tried to stop the shivering. It didn't work and her teeth chattered together.

"We're in this together," she whispered to the rat. "Shall I tell you a story?"

Even this friend deserted her. The rat scurried off at the sound of her voice. But still she spoke aloud to it, wherever it was gone, perhaps it was sat in silence in the shadows.

"Once upon a time," she said. "There was a beautiful

maid, who was locked up in the smallest dungeon of the castle for a crime she had never committed…"

She talked on, spinning the tale and wondering if there could be a happy ending to the story. Was there such a thing as a happy ending in life? For a moment her despair nearly choked her but then she remembered Valeria and hope returned, even if only a little. Her friend was safe and warm, she had happiness and Nora would bask in that knowing that one of them had got out.

The next day she was woken by the feeling of cold water poured over her face. Sputtering and miserable she came out of a disturbed sleep, to find Sophie stood over her with a bucket from which she had poured a splash.

The water soaked into Nora's hair matting it down. The cold stung her eyes and nose.

"Miss June said to wake you with the whole bucket, but I thought I'd let you see it coming," Sophie said, laughing. The rest of the bucket followed in one long freezing stream. It soaked her dress and set her shivering.

"Please," whispered Nora. "I'll freeze to death."

"You thought you were so high and mighty, did you think he'd marry you?"

"Who?"

"This gentleman Miss June hired you out to. Did you hope he'd fall in love and whisk you away? It's pathetic."

"At least Miss June had to take me away from that place. I wasn't shoved out of it like you're 'almost adoption'." Nora laughed bitterly, and Sophie smiled at her cruelly.

"See if you still think that after I tell Miss June you were cursing her name in this cupboard of yours."

"But I didn't!"

Sophie walked away with that look on her face that was part sad but mainly hate.

Miss June needed no such prompting to make Nora suffer. At least she allowed her to change into another equally thin dress, that was at least dry, if not completely clean. Nora knew she had gotten used to clean and warm clothes, and here she was back in rags.

Miss June had her haul buckets of water from the courtyard to be used by the other girls to mop up the top floor.

This floor had never been mopped before. It was the job of some of the smaller girls to sweep it twice a month but now not only did Miss June say it required mopping, but that it needed lots of full buckets.

With her back and shoulders still screaming from the whipping this was even harder than normal. Nora left her last load of two buckets and walked out the door. Miss June slammed it behind her, but Nora heard something. The buckets being emptied out a window. Now she knew this was just a trick to belittle her and to make her suffer. Putting a smile on her face she decided not to give them the satisfaction. So she returned with full ones, smiling at the two more empties waiting for their refill.

This seemed to take the wind out of Miss June's sails and there were only three more trips before the task was ended. Miss June stomped off down the corridor with the click of her boots ringing in the air.

Nora was given a half bowl of gruel for breakfast and

forced to sit and watch the others eat at lunch. In the evening she received the thinnest portion of soup, carefully drawn to avoid anything solid in the pot. She got no bread.

With this treatment she knew she would not last. So it was, she began to prepare herself to die in this place. It was not a frightening thought, far better to pass into the unknown than to live on here. She had been granted her view of the promised land and in her hubris had believed she might live there one day, gain a permanent position in Mister Richmond's home. But that was yesterday's dream, now all she wanted was warmth, a good nights sleep, and relief from the pain of the cuts and bruises on her back and shoulders.

That night she thought of the rat in the dark, even that lowest of creatures must have been happier than her. Now it was clear, there could be no happy ending for the princess in her story.

For days Miss June had her carry water for all the girls chores. It was cold out and Nora lost count of how long it had been. It might have been just one week or it could have been a month. She could feel the crawling skin of a fever, and her body was filled by some ethereal fluid that waxed hot and cold.

Each night she receded into a febrile and exhausted world in which nothing was quite real except her pain and exhaustion. Even they seemed to exist removed from her, like they were just clothes she was wearing, not really a part of her.

Every trip to the pump was the same as the last one. The blast of cold air not stopped by her thin dress. Her fingers curled around the handles. She was aware of Miss June in the corridor this time though, of Suzy saying something in the haze about a visitor. A gentleman. She heard the words "a gentleman" and reality came rushing back. She counted back on her fingers. Though it felt like months, it had just been a few days since she was brought back here. Perhaps it took him that long to wonder why she was gone, to send someone out to find her.

Miss June looked her way. The hate on her face reached new proportions, this was not anger but rage.

Nora felt life rushing back into her. He was here. It must be him. Part of her mind tried to warn her, to tell her it might be a feverish delusion, but she knew with absolute certainty.

She acted normal, dragged the bucket to the stairs. But when she heard Miss June walking away, she turned back and made her way towards the entrance hall. There were voices, she recognised Mister Richmond.

As if in a dream she tried to call out but her voice failed her. She could hear Miss June turning him away, she was too late.

She heard him refuse to leave, heard him order Miss June to produce Nora.

She was at the door and wanted to step through into the entry hall and back into the land of the living. Weakness took her and she felt herself start to faint. No, she had to hold on. Here was her chance, her hope. If she fainted away now she would never know why he came.

CHAPTER NINE

Valeria could hardly conceal her joy as she walked back with Allen. However, she did her best to mimic the wry decorum she had picked up from Miss Umbridge. Allen was constantly glancing around, as if he was about to feel the hand of the law on his neck.

Occasionally he would stop his craning and his glance would fall on her face. In these moments she got to see a huge grin crease his handsome features. It was so nice to see him and still feel the same. The black hair was still like a raven's wing. The blue eyes shone brightly. Maybe he had lost a little weight and there was a pallor to his skin but she understood that. No doubt it had always been there but at the time she would not notice , for she would share those same features. They were normal to her. Now she was used to seeing people well fed and healthy. Poor Allen was back in the life she used to lead.

Once more he glanced around and wrang his hands before him and she understood.

"You needn't worry about, Miss Umbridge," she told him. "She's got blue blood going back to the Norman Conquest — Do you know about the conquest?"

He nodded, though Valeria was not convinced. The conquest had been part of her education with Miss Umbridge and she was rather proud of this historical perspective she had gained and her own place in the vast machinery of history.

"Anyways, despite all that, she is awfully egalitarian. She quite upset Lord Ashton at dinner a few days ago by holding him up for almost an hour while she chatted with the chimney sweeps who were cleaning out her flue."

"She sounds like a real gent," Allen said smiling at her again.

Whenever he smiled, Valeria felt that little skip in her heart. Allen was safe! Allen was here.

The walk back was one of the most joyful she had ever enjoyed. The sun was setting as they walked, painting the sky in beautiful pinks and purples.

"Tell me what you've been doing with yourself, Allen. Have you a home? Is picking pockets your only work?"

"Not exactly, though none of it's as legitimate as you might hope." His shoulders dropped and he seemed to shrink a little.

"I understand," she managed though there was a lump in her throat. How she wanted him to have a home just like her.

"I work for a crook who keeps a number of petty criminals like me in business. We give him a cut of what we steal and he fences it, provides safe sleeping quarters, and finds us jobs to do."

"So you weren't going to keep that purse, but give it to some criminal slumlord?"

"No... he owns a small house... it's not kept in the best condition. But he has a cat to keep the rats out and he cooks up a fine stew. We do alright, I rarely go to bed hungry now... But no, that purse would have gone to him. Though not before I squirreled a few coins away. I'm saving see, to get out. I want to leave London, to buy a cart, or sell something, maybe I'd get a shoeshine boy to work for me. Though, I don't know if I dare."

"Why not?" she asked.

"Abe... my benefactor... he isn't the kind to let his employees go easily. We all owe him something and when we pay it off, he thinks of something else we owe him. To be honest..." He glanced about again as if looking for his benefactor on this very road. "... I'm a little terrified of him."

"You keep looking about, was he there, at the market?"

"Yes, he's been teaching me to cut purses and wanted to see what I've learned. I really shouldn't have slipped away like this, but it doesn't look like he saw me leave. It will be alright. He'll be angry when I get back, especially cos I'm empty handed, but I think he'll understand... when I tell him it was about a girl."

Valeria blushed.

"Why do you fear him so."

"Well, it is nothing concrete, but I do suspect that he might have more on his conscience than theft. A couple of boys have left since I started work with him and he always has a story. They went to sea, were apprenticed to a blacksmith up North, or came down with the cholera. That sort of thing. But there was one boy, he was very young... he had no talent for picking pockets and was eating Taylor's bread every day. That's one thing he mentions if you don't pull your weight. Anyway, one day this boy is gone. Taylor says, very casual like, the boy is now working happily as a barrow boy in Portsmouth."

Valeria felt sick, knowing what was coming. "Oh dear, what did you hear? Is he alright?"

"Hear? Nothing. I saw it with my own eyes. Two days later I see a beggar boy who looks rather like the missing lad. So I sidle up to pass him a copper but he doesn't see me. I'm stood right in front of him and he can't see me because some beast has clawed his eyes out, or burnt them, or something. There are just these two red holes in his face..."

Valeria felt sick, the beautiful evening seemed to take on a terrible sinister pall and she began looking about as if Taylor might be hunting her too. How could she let Allen go back to this when she had a warm bed and a caring home to go to?

"I walked away without saying a word. I could have been mistaken, and I've not seen the lad about again. Maybe I just made a mistake. His face was changed a lot, you know. Twas not just the eyes, there were other scars. But, it made me wonder about all those other boys who quit and went on to better things, what if they didn't?"

Valeria wanted to cry, she couldn't understand how Allen was able to be so calm about something so horrible. Or how he could go back to this man each night.

"I've frightened you. I'm sorry," he said. "Forgive me, it was just a little joke to make my life sound more like an adventure. It was a story, like Nora used to tell."

Valeria looked at him, unsure which story to believe. Was he sparing her? He seemed genuine. Never mind then. "Let's change the subject," she said. "Do you remember..." she asked him about the good times they shared for what she felt was the hundredth time, and of course he did, and so they walked on in each other's cheerfulness.

He helped her over the stile as they approached Miss Umbridge's house and she felt his hands, stronger now, more like a man's on her waist and she felt something thrill in her. Though she couldn't quite tell what.

How she wanted to tell him everything she had learned, but the walk was too short and she had barely got past volume one of Rome's rise and fall when they found themselves in the kitchen.

Cook took the duck in a flurry of curses.

"That Mister Wright is early, Valeria. Do hurry and take that bottle of claret up to them. I'll get this duck roasting." Her plump hands were already preparing the duck and you could feel the heat from the oven.

"Who is this then?" Cook asked but kept talking before they could reply. "No, no time for introductions, don't spring him on Mister Wright now, he's not so welcoming as our Deloris..."

Valeria felt her self smile once more. Cook was such a good soul. She was still talking to herself, the oven and the duck as Valeria left, carefully holding the corkscrew and bottle with Allen behind her.

"Now, let me make the introductions, Allen. You bow to Miss Umbridge and if Mister Wright offers his hand you shake it. If not, it is a bow for him too." She looked at Allen, whose face looked rather worried. He'd grown into even more of a good looking chap.

"Oh, I've done all the talking. Once Miss Umbridge has approved of you, we'll find you a bed and you can tell me everything."

"Ah... yes. Everything. Though I really must be go—"

Valeria cut him off and opened the door to the library and ignoring Cook's command she immediately imposed Allen on Mister Wright.

Allen performed marvellously, bowing to Miss Umbridge, speaking strongly and clearly. Valeria could almost see him as one of them, if his clothes weren't so scrappy and his accent so cockney. He did look good though, like a prince in pauper's clothes he had that way about him, a bit of swagger like he was meant to be there as much as they were.

Mister Wright seemed about to shake Allen's hand, but he glanced at Valeria catching her eye. His expression changed quite suddenly. She steeled herself for his usual probing stare at the rest of her body, but this time he seemed to be studying her face. She glanced at Allen then back at him and Mister Wright retracted his hand.

Allen, whose hand was already out smirked defiantly and bowed over elaborately, putting one arm out and almost touching his knees with his chin. The effect was, after his elegant bob to Miss Umbridge, decidedly mocking, but nothing actionable.

"What is your relation with Miss Collins then, Mister...?"

"Just Allen, no family to speak of so no family name to speak of. I'm a blank slate. My relationship with Valeria here goes back a long time. Childhood friends we were a few years back, but circumstances came between us. Pure coincidence put me in her orbit this afternoon and we have been making up for lost time."

"Childhood friends? You hardly seem as though childhood has ended. Might I ask your age, Mister Allen?"

"You may ask away, Mister Thomas." He turned to Miss Umbridge. "I can't thank you enough for letting me in. I fear I am not really dressed for such high company."

Mister Wright, with a sour look on his face suggested they go into dinner.

Since Allen was Valeria's guest, she too was invited to the table and Mister Wright stepped forward firmly offering her his arm, taking her away from Allen, and escorting her to the table from the library.

Allen, in almost perfect mockery of him, offered his arm similarly to Miss Umbridge who laughed delightedly. "How inappropriate, Mister Allen," she said in a voice that suggested that "inappropriate" was the greatest virtue imaginable in an act. She hung off his arm like a debutante with the village rake.

Allen shone at the table; where the prospect of condescending patronage seemed to have made him uncomfortable, the outright hostility from Mister

Wright seemed to imbue him with a kind of energy. Valeria could only imagine what had happened to turn the young scamp into such a confident young man. He seemed unperturbed by the difference in class and spoke directly to Miss Umbridge and Mister Wright without a hint of her reverence.

He was not rude, at least not explicitly, though Mister Wright was the brunt of much subtle mockery, but nor did he kowtow to his host or her guest.

I suppose he feels more comfortable fighting these upper-class types, thought Valeria.

It made her feel rather ashamed. She had become a pet to the rich and powerful so easily. Miss Umbridge was truly kind to her, but did not see her as an equal. There was in the two men's combative attitude an inherent egalitarianism, though she could not for the life of her understand what made Mister Wright so cold towards Allen who had done him no offence.

It wasn't pride, for he talked with Cook and Valeria as friends and equals, though Valeria did her best to respect the separation. Since their first meeting, despite his repeated insistence, she refused to call him Thomas. She still found being alone in a room with him to be a frightening experience. The hunger in his face haunted her and seemed to turn him from an otherwise attractive man into something like a cat stalking a mouse.

Miss Umbridge seemed fascinated by Allen who told her a few stories of living on the street, carefully glossing over the more criminal aspects of his life. He slurped his soup and when the duck came ate the meat with his hands at first, until Valeria kicked him under the table.

The whole meal seemed to take an eternity, and Valeria longed to get him alone so they could catch up, and conspire as they had when they were both so much younger. She wanted so much to hold his hand again, to hide away somewhere and just be herself with him.

She was also aware that he seemed more charming now he'd grown up a little, and he certainly seemed more handsome. Mister Wright might have given him some competition but his face was curled into a most unappealing expression of contempt and irritation. He looked in fact like he might need to be sick.

Thoughts like this dogged her all through the meal; as she watched the faces of her table mates, she longed to be able to hear Allen's thoughts and discuss their future, if they had any.

CHAPTER TEN

*C*hrist, this man's an arse, Allen thought as he listened to Mister Wright telling an *amusing* anecdote to Valeria. It was about some tenant of his who would eat nothing but cheese. Apparently, he had driven paying renters out of the other rooms in this property with the smell of it.

"I'm rather fond of a good cheese myself, Mister Wright," he said, careful not to let his smirk taint the tone of respect in his voice. "Although, I am surprised that a man who keeps such small rooms as you are describing would be able to afford such a quantity of cheese. I tend to find the landlords of London always do their damnedest to squeeze their renters dry."

"I offer a rather fairer rate than most," Mister Wright said his eyes widening at the need to defend himself.

"I wonder then that you lost so many renters to the merest whiff of cheese. Are you sure the smell was coming from the larder and not the open sewer on that street?"

The blow landed hard, Mister Wright flinched. It was clear that he did not like being embarrassed like that. Though it intrigued Allen to note that his irritation was not at being mocked before his employer but Valeria.

So that's how it is, Allen thought, unaccountably furious, though careful not to allow that anger to cross his face.

Miss Umbridge leaned across the table and replenished his plate with potatoes and some more duck.

"You look half starved, Mister Allen. You must eat up. Would you care for a little more claret?"

"Thank you, Ma'am," Allen said, spearing a potato whole on his fork and taking a bite. "It might be a little while before I eat this well again, after all."

"I imagine duck is harder to come by than cheese in your line of work," said Mister Wright. "You haven't really told us what that is?"

Allen looked over at Valeria and winked, then, flashing what he thought of as his most charming smile he replied. "Oh, this and that, Mister Wright. I have fingers in many pies in the city, but I think it is rather uncouth to talk business at the dinner table. I'd far rather hear about this Pliny fellow Miss Umbridge was talking about. Is he a friend of yours?"

Mister Wright couldn't resist the bait and in rather pompous tones corrected Allen, and to his great pleasure he heard Valeria laugh. After all, it was she who had been telling him about Pliny the Roman and his boat Here they were, sharing a little joke, while Mister Wright made a fool of himself by missing the gag entirely.

He was was pleased to find, the more he watched Valeria and Mister Wright interact that Mister Wright's intentions were clearly his own alone. In fact, Valeria seemed cold towards him in a way he had never seen her be cold to anyone before.

He shook his head.

You damn fool, he thought, *you hardly know her, haven't seen her in years and you pretend to know her habits. For all you know she is cold as the moon to everybody but yourself, cook and Umbridge.*

After dinner, Valeria begged him to stay, begging him not to go. She seemed terrified that he would disappear again completely. Mister Wright seemed to note her desire for Allen to stay, which was clearly annoying him greatly.

Despite her protestations, Allen insisted he really had to go. He knew Taylor would already be furious at him for having given him the slip back at the market, and then doubly furious at him for having stayed out so late.

Valeria reluctantly led him through Miss Umbridge's opulence into the hallway where she opened the door for him. She fetched his hat down from the stand and instead of handing it to him, she put it on his head. He felt her hands adjust it, her wrists enclosing his head like a bracket. He looked at her as she concentrated on setting his cap at just the right jaunty angle and thought to himself, that she was every bit as beautiful as he remembered. Just as beautiful as he had thought to himself every night since that witch, Miss June, had caught them together in the dark of the orphanage.

She was like a candle in the dark, chasing away something... some discomfort he hadn't known was there. Like an itch that went unnoticed till it was scratched. He smiled and their eyes met.

They stood there in the doorway looking at each other and he felt some great force reach out of the dark outside. It seemed to be pushing him, compelling him to do or say something, but he didn't know what. He hesitated and the moment passed.

"Must be going, but may I call on you here again some time?"

"Oh, Allen. You absolutely must."

She smiled that sweet smile at him and took the door holding it open until he had reached the street, only closing it after he turned back to give her a wave.

The door closing plunged the drive into a gloom and he set off down towards the main gate. It would be a long walk back to Taylor's place. Not a pleasant one, as he could just imagine what Taylor would have to say.

"Had fun cavorting with your little miss there, Allen?" Taylor's voice carried from ahead of him in the dark. For a moment, Allen thought his own mind was playing tricks on him but as he walked forward he could make out Taylor leaning on the gatepost in the dark.

"Taylor, you scared me half to death loitering there. I hope I didn't cause you too much worry slipping off like that."

"It is Mister Taylor to you on a day like today. Slipping off, boy? You'd have to try a little harder to lose old Abel. I followed you here all the way, and have been waiting about ever since. It wasn't too bad earlier when there were folks about but St. Mary's has rung the hour at least three times since it got dark. I thought maybe you really had given me the slip."

"I hope it wasn't too much of an inconvenience for you?"

"No, my boy. No trouble at all, so long as something came of it. You meet the old widow?"

"Yes. She's a rather pleasant old bird actually."

"I'm sure she is. Rich too. I hadn't realised this was old Miss Umbridge's house. Lot of money that old lady has. Lot of bank drafts, bonds, and the like. Valuable as gold but nothing like the weight. A good mark, boy. Well done."

Taylor's meaning now clear, Allen felt the need to assert himself.

"I wasn't hunting a mark, Taylor. I was visiting an old friend—"

"Is that the tasty young serving girl you picked up in the market? Your 'old friend'?"

Taylor's tone was getting under Allen's skin. There was something threatening in in it along with a smug satisfaction that suggested he was withholding some vital trump card waiting for Allen to make him play.

"That's right and I'd ask you to show some respect when you speak of Miss Valeria."

"Miss Valeria. She looked worth a penny or two herself. If you were to pay by the hour."

"I asked you to show—"

"You asked, and I declined." Taylor's face went hard

his tone matched. "I pay your board, I feed you, I've taught you a trade or two and shared my own profits with you along the way. That is called investment. And something you need to understand about an investment is that it needs to show a profit at some point."

"I have made you more cutting purses than you've ever shared with me."

"Aye, but I can pick a pocket myself, I can't get myself access to an old lady who always keeps her some valuables on her premises in a wooden desk under lock and key. You been in the library boy?"

"Yes. Hang on. How do you know all this?"

"Because that condescending old bag talks to everyone and everyone talks to old Taylor. Like I said, I been stuck out here waiting for you but I haven't been twirling my thumbs. I have been chatting with every passerby who cares to gossip and gossip they do. So you've been in the library."

"Aye." Allen was beginning to feel sick. "But I won't go back to rob Valeria's house."

"Oh, Allen. You'll do as I say because you are not my

only investment."

"So what, you'll send someone else?"

"Maybe, maybe they'll break that desk and steal the ladies... 'financial instruments' is what the haberdasher said. Money's for the poor like you and me. Company bonds are what the rich deal in. Better than a banknote, for a bond pays interest."

"You wouldn't!"

Taylor laughed a cold sound that echoed in the night. "Maybe they'll break the desk. So what? A broken desk, maybe that's too risky, they'll make that call. But know this, boy. If I send a man into that house, and that man isn't you, he will maybe break the desk... but without the slightest doubt, they will definitely break Miss Valeria. Starting with her teeth, perhaps an arm or a rib. It might not stop there. Some of the fellas I've invested in are real cutthroat types, others have proclivities that would make you shake to your core, little Allen. Anything could happen to your girl... anything. So tell me then, am I going to send you for those papers, or am I going to send someone else?" A calloused and dirty hand reached out and pointed at the house and then back at Allen.

Allen's heart sank, how could he betray Valeria by stealing from the home she lived in? How could he betray her by letting Taylor send a thug after her? That hand reached out of the darkness again and gestured at him.

Could he make her leave, get her to hide out? What kind of life would that be for her? Besides, would she ever forgive him for bringing something like this down on her new and perfect life?

No. There was only one thing for it. He would simply have to do his best to get in there. Steal perhaps just enough of these bonds to satisfy Taylor's desire to rise up in the world and leave without a trace. Perhaps no one would notice. Miss Umbridge seemed so rich she might not notice a few hundred pounds missing here or there.

Feeling sick and furious all at the same time, Allen drew in a deep breath. From the look on Taylor's face he knew what Allen's answer was before he said it.

"I'll do it," he said. "And if you do a damn thing to Valeria, you'll find out whether or not I have it in me to be one of your cutthroats."

CHAPTER ELEVEN

William Richmond struck the door of the orphanage with the head of his cane enjoying the authoritative thwack of it. He couldn't help but note that the lead paint on the door needed sprucing up. The heavy oak door was showing through and where he struck it a large flake of the paint jumped loose.

The head of the cane was sterling silver and the cane had been his father's. Rapping its now unpolished head against things was an oddly satisfying affront to the memory of the mean old man.

It had been four days since Miss June had turned up at the house and rushed young Nora away. Four days in which he had found himself deeply bothered by her absence and by the rising tide of mess that encroached on his work. It wouldn't have mattered much, he kept telling himself, but if he ran out of glassware or the animals went unfed he lost valuable research time.

It took him one solar cycle to decide that he needed Nora back and another hour and a half to persuade Stephen to go to the orphanage before preparing dinner. When he had come back empty handed he'd decided firmly to go himself, but something seemed to shame him a little.

What the reason could possibly be for his embarrassment was beyond him. She had been a useful house girl; so of course he felt her absence. There could be nothing more to it.

No other reason he missed her.

Maids came and went without him noticing much but these few days without Nora about had felt oddly uncomfortable. She was so easy to talk to, so eager to hear about his experiments and although she understood but half of what he talked about that alone was an improvement. Already, she had learned a great deal from when she started. Then, she had appeared not to understand any of his rambling talk of science. Now she could occasionally discuss it with him.

That must be it. His ego. Self-preening. No wonder he was embarrassed. With that settled he had taken himself off on the first day, after wringing the address out of Stephen and had taken a hansom cab around to Miss June's charitable venture.

He rapped on the door again and this time it opened in front of him and a girl of about eight or nine — or perhaps a very malnourished twelve, he had read recently some fascinating studies on how starvation affected the development of the young — opened the door and asked politely for his name.

He handed her his calling card and asked to see Miss June.

"I can't read, Sir," she said.

"Not to worry, lass. You take that to Miss June, she will be able to read it for herself."

"Yes, Sir."

Rather than offer him a place to wait the young girl closed the door and scurried off into the old building.

The street it fronted looked murky and cold despite the noonday sun, all smogged over greys and black puddles of foul smelling water.

He stood watching an old carter whipping his donkey along the road despite neither him nor the donkey seeming to be in much hurry. It seemed a senseless act, more habit than maliciousness on the part of the carter. The two of them, man and beast, traipsed their way down the otherwise empty street, past his hansom and up towards the river.

Eventually the door reopened, and the young girl reappeared, allowing him into the gloomy hallway. It was darker and colder in here even than on the street. Though nothing was quite as cold as Miss June's expression as she stood there.

"To what do I owe this visit, Sir?" she asked with a barely concealed hostility.

"Nora has failed to turn up to do the work I paid you for," William said, trying out a smile on her and attempting to keep his voice cheery.

He could hardly believe anyone lived in this building. It was clean to be sure, and the noises of industry came from within, but it seemed dead. The cold and dark made it feel like a prison, unliveable. Somehow he now knew that Nora had lied about her circumstances and a deep shame came over him, he should have seen through it.

"I am sure you are not so dishonest a person as to take a man's money and then fail to provide the service for which it was exchanged. That might be reason for me to seek out the constables, there are plenty of cells in the debtor's prison. I imagine someone in your line of business might be more aware than most of what it would be like to be a resident in such a place."

"Your threat does not frighten me, Sir. Nora no longer works for you. Nor will any of my girls," Miss June said, her back straight her face one of disapproval. "And your fee was paid on the basis of you treating my girls appropriately not coddling them with tea and cakes."

"There were no cakes," Mister Richmond firmly said. "Nor any coddling. She was taking a well-earned break from her work before finishing her shift, which — I might add — you have already taken a fee for."

"Cake or no, I know when a man is giving a girl airs and making an offer of vice to her."

"Might I ask what I have done to offend? I have certainly done nothing that might hurt Nora. Certainly not more than you could by keeping her in a sty like this and without the slightest doubt I am guilty of no vice apart from the occasional pinch of snuff and a once weekly overindulgence in a porter stout of which I am uncommonly fond."

"Offend? I wouldn't presume to tell you how to live your life, Mister Richmond, but I will not allow my wards to be drawn into your degradation. Porter stout indeed, that's a fine word for it. I have known men like you, have been used cruelly myself by men like you, and I will not give you the comfort or use of my girls. If not for their irredeemable souls then for my own." This speech was delivered with all the venom of an adder, but without even a hint of anger, nothing but disgust showed on the old crone's face.

"I feel that I am being accused of something, but am unsure exactly what, Miss June. Nora has been invaluable as a maid and a most polite and companionable presence in my household. That presence is missed. I will have her finish out her contract."

"Aye, a companionable presence no doubt. The little hussy might have the appetite for it but I do not. I will not hire her to you, contract or no."

The words used sent a spark of anger into his stomach which grew to such an extent he wondered if he could do an experiment to prove it. Hussy indeed! "That is it, Miss June. I am not looking to hire her anymore. I am looking to take her into my household staff on a permanent basis. The institution of slavery was made illegal in this country in 1807 and as to your accusations regarding my conduct I hope you are aware of the slander laws, which are a damn sight older than that."

William took a breath, he had to remain in control. However, this woman's accusations and impertinent tone were beginning to wear on his patience and he was increasingly concerned about Nora's wellbeing in a house like this. The spark had turned into a growing anger and indignation. It was not dignified to lose one's temper but damn it if he wasn't being sorely tried.

"You are looking to get a beating, young man. I will not be ordered about by anyone, no matter how high and mighty, within the walls of my own home."

"This hovel you run is no home, Miss June. It appears little more than a prison in which you profit by the misery of the inmates. Fetch Nora and we will leave it to her to decide her fate. I will be gone with her if she wishes to come. If she really does feel safe locked up in your gaol, then I will take my leave of both of you and never darken your already pitch black doorway again. Fetch her. Now."

"I'm here already."

He turned to see Nora in the doorway to his left. She walked carefully as if something hurt her when she moved and her dress was in tatters. Her hair was lank and unwashed and there was blood coming from a callous on her right hand.

"I didn't believe it when Suzy said you'd come. It is most pleasant to see you again, Sir," she said, her voice little more than a whisper.

Mister Richmond saw in her eyes some terrible animal fear, and also a look of hope. It made him feel like her protector. Like he were a raft in a storm and she a sailor loosed on the waves.

Miss June took two steps over to Nora and before he could do anything she struck the girl hard in the face.

"I will whip you within an inch, you little tart," she screamed. "Get back to your room. You will not speak to this... *gentleman* again."

It took several tries and a viciously scratched face for William to get his hands on Miss June's wrists and pull her away from Nora. With a firm grip on the old lady he addressed Nora alone.

"If you would care for it, there is a permanent position in my household, Miss Nora. This is your choice, not mine and not this old Harpy's. If you wish to, there is a hansom cab waiting outside. I doubt you have much to bring from this place but you may collect anything you need."

For a moment his heart hung in the balance, terrified that she would choose to stay here and leave him to — to what exactly? he wondered. Why was he the one afraid when Nora had so much more to oppress her mind.

"Thank you, Sir," Nora said and curtseyed. His heart lifted and hands loosened slightly.

Miss June took her opportunity. The blow was not hard but struck him in a tender place, the pain shot through him like a bolt and he found himself off balance while the old woman scratched again at his eyes.

He backed away, unwilling to fend the old lady off and possibly hurt her but in considerable pain. There came the sound of a colossal wallop and the noise stopped. Miss June stood there utterly stunned. Nora was between her and William. There was a bright red mark on the old grey face of Miss June. Nora had slapped her.

The shock on Miss June's face was total. Her eyes were bulging out of her head in astonishment.

Taking this moment, Nora turned and grabbed his hand pulling him towards the door.

Trying to reassert himself he put an arm around her shoulder to shelter her on the street, but she seemed to have grown vastly in strength since she slapped the old woman. She stood taller than he had ever seen her before even without her shoes and he realised how cowed she had been by the bleakness of this place.

She looked at him and smiled as he helped her into the carriage, though she hardly needed it. It was as if the sickness he had seen on her when she came into the hallway had been left there. Even in her rags she looked almost regal. He wanted to kneel and kiss her feet.

Despite the runnels of blood making their way down his face from the scratches, he was smiling too.

Nora would be with him now and safe. He felt light, airy, in a way he had not in years.

How odd, he thought. I wonder what the reason for such joyous emotion is?

He found himself talking excitedly on the way. He wrapped his coat about her although she didn't seem cold and told her of what she had missed. That one of the monkey's was pregnant. That he had been sent a half dozen new species of orchids from an expedition to Madagascar. She seemed to be only half-listening, but he couldn't help himself, he was excited to see her and excited to tell someone about the work he had being doing.

The only time she really studied him closely was to wipe the blood off his face. It had hardened to little flecks, almost like the paint on the door. He hadn't really noticed. It was only then that the scratches Miss June had given him began to hurt.

CHAPTER TWELVE

*W*hat was that?

Valeria woke in a sudden rush of consciousness. One moment she was dreaming, the next she was in her room, immediately awake in the near pitch black. Unsure what had woken her but sure that whatever it was deserved her full and rather highly strung attention.

A pulse beat in her throat and neck as her heart hammered in her chest. The two of them were so loud that she could hardly hear. Still, she tried to reach out with her ears to touch the sounds of the night.

The house often creaked at night when it cooled and

every sound became the footstep of a murderer looking to bleed the whole household dry for some dark Satanic purpose.

She had been dreaming of the passage in the Odyssey where the Cyclops takes the wine from Odysseus not knowing that the wine is part of Odysseus' plan to escape the Cyclops' home. Odysseus' speech had stuck in her memory as she read it, there was something horrible in the deception, even knowing the Cyclops' own horrific crimes:

"Cyclops, take a bowl of wine from my hand," Odysseus had said. "That may make way for the man's flesh thou hast eat, and show what drink our ship held; which in sacred vow I offer to thee to take ruth on me in my dismission home. Thy rages be now no more sufferable. How shall men, Mad and inhuman that thou art, again Greet thy abode, and get thy actions grace, If thus thou ragest, and eat'st up their race."

Was that a scraping sound? She thought she could hear glass tinkling against glass and with great trepidation she put her foot down on the wooden floor and rose to her feet. The gentle rustle of nightgown in the dark seemed loud enough to betray her presence and she froze for a moment. Maybe there was no one there, maybe this was just a dream.

Only she felt it was more and crept across the room. The corridor was lit by the moon coming through a window at the end of it, and by its light she found some matches and a taper.

I dare not light it yet, she thought. *It might alert the intruder... No, there is no intruder. Just the sounds of an old house on a cold night and the beating of my own terrified heart.*

Her breath formed a ghostly mist in front of her with each breath and she moved through it silent as a spirit. Still, she listened closely, as if some noise might bring her back from this dream to the land of the living. This then must be the witching hour.

She began to whisper the passage from Homer again: "Cyclops, take a bowl of wine from my hand, that may make way for the man's flesh thou hast eat, and show what drink our ship held..."

At the stairs she paused and listened. It was much clearer now. There was definitely someone moving around down there. Probably just Cook making a midnight snack, else someone had left the latch up and the dog had got in.

Despite her reassurances she continued downstairs with caution, adjusting her footing to avoid any stair that gave off a creak when she stepped on it. Down she went into the belly of the house.

"And show what drink our ship held, which in sacred vow I offer to thee to take ruth on me in my dismission home."

There was the noise again, she paused trying to work out where it was. Not the kitchen, so not Cook. Nor the conservatory, so not the dog. Then what? A shiver ran down her spine.

"Thy rages be now no more sufferable. How shall men, Mad and inhuman that thou art, again..."

She heard it again, this time the sound of a drawer opening. It was from the library.

With quick, light steps Valeria sneaked up to the door. The handle turned in her hand and suddenly there was the bang of the over-sprung bolt. It sent a shock of fear through her like electricity and she immediately knew what had woken her up. That familiar sound at an unfamiliar time.

"Greet thy abode, and get thy actions grace, if thus thou ragest, and eat'st up their race."

She threw the door open and her heart dropped, it wasn't fear she felt, it was fury. Anger at being betrayed for there, frozen over open drawers of Miss Umbridge's desk, was Allen. His face was one of hangdog shame.

"Val—" he began.

She didn't let him finish, advancing on him with the unlit taper pointed like a sword she heard herself say in a voice far louder than she intended, "Is this what you meant by 'calling on me again'? What the hell do you think you are doing? I... I trusted you. I brought you into my home. How could you do this to me?"

"I didn't want to. But I had to."

"No, you did not, Allen. You could have robbed anyone else. Or even better, you could have curled up in a gutter and died."

"Shhh, please, Valeria. I can explain. They threatened..."

"Don't you dare, 'shhh' me, you rotten liar. I thought you cared about me." She was screaming now and wanted to stop, but the emotions she felt, the hurt, the anger, drove the words out of her louder and louder. "I wanted you back in my life for so long. I missed you and now you do this."

"Please, Valeria, let me."

She grabbed an account book from one of the open drawers and drew back her hand to throw it at him, when the bolt on the door banged again.

"What in God's name is going on, Valeria." The voice was Deloris' and Valeria lowered her throwing arm.

Allen froze for a moment. Then with astonishing speed, shot across the room, and planting a foot on a plant stand, he got his hands on the high window sill above it. Cook burst in after Deloris and ran across the room after him. But her fingers closed on cold air as Allen rolled through the narrow window and into the flower beds outside.

There was a long silence in which Valeria looked to the window, to Cook, to Deloris, to the open desk drawers, then to the private account book in her own hand. The story it told seemed clear as day to her and seemed to be dawning on Cookie and Miss Umbridge too.

Miss Umbridge looked deeply pained, as if she had been physically hurt during the whole debacle. Cook on the other looked ready to deal out some physical hurt of her own.

"No," said Valeria, heart falling. "You can't think...?"

"I most certainly do think, Miss Collins."

Valeria wanted to cry, this was the first time since they had first met that Miss Umbridge has spoken to her in this way. The old lady looked like she was close to tears as well.

"What else am I to think? Your little friend of childhood, whose praises you sang and who you brought to my door, showed about my house, and then brought to this room in the middle of the night. Look at you, you are holding my personal papers in your very hand."

"No, I was going to hit him with them," but she realised as she heard them how weak an excuse it sounded, how transparent a lie despite its concrete truth. "I came down and found him here—"

"As planned, no doubt," Cook said.

She looked around somehow hoping Allen would still be there. That he might explain the situation, but no, she was alone. He had abandoned her again, only this time it was his betrayal not Sophie's. The pain came bubbling up in deep loud sobs.

"I found him here. I tried to stop him. I didn't know. I would never."

She felt cut off.

"I want you out of my house. For the service you have done me these last years I won't set the police on you, but if I ever see you again I will have you sent to the dock. Do not test me, Valeria."

Valeria looked to Cook, praying for an ally. Cook's initial anger seemed to have waned and she was looking at Valeria rather pityingly. "Do you believe me, Cook?"

At the look on the woman's face she sank to her knees.

"Well, I don't know," Cook said. "Sure enough it don't look right, but looks can deceive, as the good Lord himself says." She looked to Miss Umbridge with a considered glance. "I wouldn't go so far as to tell you what to do in your own home, Miss Umbridge. But this just doesn't seem like our Valeria's kind of plan. Surely, she knew the boy that done it, but she was the one screaming fit to bring the house down, and she was holding that book an awful lot like she might be about to strike the boy…"

Miss Umbridge looked a little less sure of herself, and a little less hurt.

"Please believe me," Valeria whispered. "This is the only place I've ever been happy. I would never do anything to jeopardise that or to hurt either of you. I feel as betrayed as you. Allen was my friend and he broke into my home. Because that's what this place is to me. A home. I'm sorry I brought him in, but I never thought he would do this to me, to you, to this house."

Miss Umbridge took all this in with a look on her face that seemed to seal Valeria's fate, but when she opened her mouth to speak she said, "You may stay, Valeria. For tonight at least. It is late, and I have just been terrified by an intruder. Cook, get the Peelers in to look all this over. Valeria, you are to give them a full description of your friend when they get here. I will sleep on this and decide what to do with you in the morning. Whatever happens, I will be keeping a close eye on you in future, young Valeria."

She turned and went up the stairs, the light of her candle fading as she did so. Valeria was left with Cook and the wreckage left behind by Allen.

"Come, lass, let's get you a cup of tea. I'll send the gardener's boy to the constables."

Valeria moved through the house as if in a dream. In the warmth of the kitchen where a low coal fire burned perpetually her breath no longer had the ghostly air. Everything felt solid again, every edge seemed sharp enough to cut, every surface hard enough to bruise. It was all realer than real.

Cook sat her down and they waited for the police. Cook talked a little about nothing much, set about preparing for tomorrow's meals. "Might as well use the time if we're to be kept up by state inquiries."

Sad beyond words Valeria told them of her meeting with Allen, leaving out that he had picked her pocket. She gave them some details changing the colour of his hair and eyes a little and hoping that he might never be seen again, by the police, but especially by herself.

For too long she had hoped things might come right with her old friends, that Allen and Nora would be well. It had been a childish way of going through life.

As she spoke to the police officers her mind wandered, she remembered Mister Wright's attention and wondered if perhaps there was anything to them, any substance. He was no saint to be sure, but better to know a man's villainy than to be caught by surprise as Allen had done to her.

The officers eventually bid them all good night and told Cook that they would keep an eye out for this scallywag. That they would ask about the place, but that these things rarely resulted in much if the villain wasn't caught in the act.

Cook apologised profusely for having let him get away and gave Valeria a meaningful look that Valeria noted. She just wanted to go back to bed, to lie down, and to cry in privacy.

After what seemed like another age, with the faint

glimmer of sunrise coming up over the horizon Valeria made her way back to her room and fell into bed.

Although exhausted she couldn't sleep. She lay there with her eyes fixed on the ceiling.

She imagined Allen running through the dark, bounding over the low wall at the end of the garden and tearing off towards the lights of the city. She wondered what he was thinking. He had betrayed her to be sure, but she couldn't just throw him away from her heart. Surely, he must have had his reasons. Perhaps he could use the money he took to get away from that man who may or may not have blinded children to make them beg for him when pickpocketing failed.

That was a fearful thought, Allen hadn't got away with much. Maybe a few sheets of paper. If it wasn't as much as his employer expected, would he be similarly altered, perhaps docked a limb in order to beg as a veteran of the colonial wars?

She wished now she had given the police his employer's name. She had thought she was protecting him. Now she wondered if, instead, she had condemned him to a fate far worse than prison time, or even the noose.

But maybe it was all exactly as it seemed: Allen had betrayed her, Miss Umbridge would throw her out in an instant if she decided that Valeria had, after all, been a part of Allen's crime. The image of having to return to the orphanage in disgrace came to her in vivid colour. Or worse, she was almost old enough for the workhouse to take her.

She'd seen the women, old before their time, worked to death for being too poor to keep a home. The tears fell freely, this time at least her sobs were silent, shared only with the voiceless ceiling above her.

How close everything was to total collapse, how close it had always been to total collapse. She had been a fool to believe that life could get better, that it could stay that way. Hadn't Miss June told her, that life for girls like her, always ended in pain?

CHAPTER THIRTEEN

*N*ora was in shock. She'd struck Miss June and run out of the orphanage. The rest of it felt like a dream, as if it were all happening to someone else. The hansom cab had pulled away and William had said something to her that she didn't hear. It was only when she realised he was bleeding that she seemed able to bring herself back to the cab.

Now she sat in a chair, in the servants quarters, while Stephen warmed some brandy and cloves in a saucepan for her.

What had she done? Her whole life, from her mother's passing til now had been lived under Miss

June's roof, under her control. For so long, she had longed to escape but now it all seemed so overwhelming. Where before there had been harsh certainties now she faced the terror of the unknown.

Nora had been dreadfully cruel to Miss June, for all her bitterness and hardness, Miss June had been the woman who raised her. Despite everything, her loss was felt... for now as fear.

She said as much to Stephen who looked over from the saucepan the harsh expression dropping from his face. "We often feel that way when someone raised us. But that Miss June, she used you and your friends. She squeezed all she could out of you and was ready to consign you to the workhouse or the hospital or even — from the look of how we found you — a pauper's grave. You don't owe her anything, least of all your love."

Nora nodded, she knew he was right... but she also knew for all the horror of that place, there had been joy to be had, surely. Now there was nothing but the terror of the unknown.

Suddenly, she could hear Miss June talking, "If there

are a myriad of paths then some will lead to salvation as surely as some will to destruction."

"Now child, drink this." Stephen handed her a tin mug from which came the biting smell of liquor and spices. His face was back to its usual scowl but he sat next to her and looked at her very carefully as she sipped.

"How are you, Nora? You look like you've seen the land of the dead and are only partly returned from it."

"I feel that way a little, Stephen. I feel..." but she couldn't find the words and fell silent. Her eyes fell to her lap where the mug was cradled. She took another sip. It was good, the alcohol bit at her throat as it went down, but the warmth it brought with it spread from her stomach almost immediately. She smiled a little, felt hopeful once more.

"What is to become of me, Stephen?"

"Best I let Mister Richmond give you those details, since it was his hare-brained scheme to break you out of that vile institution. I best go prep your room for you. Finish that up now, all of it, it will give you some strength."

Taking another sip, she watched Stephen walk off and smiled to herself. Earlier he had given her some chicken broth filled with pieces of meat. It was hearty and filled her stomach warming her from within but the chill had returned. The new drink contained booze, and it was taking the edge off the pain from her back and shoulders. They were still bruised and cut from where Miss June had made the girls cane her for a half-dozen imagined infractions since— My God, she thought. It's only been four days.

Four days between Miss June's inopportune arrival during her and William — Mr Richmond's -- teatime and the dramatic events of today. It seemed like a lifetime. Sophie had crowed for days at her suffering, consolidating her place as the oldest girl in the orphanage who wasn't in disgrace.

Four days of beatings and half-rations, of the bucket and stairs. She had not been allowed to wash once in that time and had her shoes taken away from her. She had even been given the most ratty dress, all to *teach her humility*. But what had really hurt all that time was knowing that she would never see William again.

Only, she had been wrong about that, wrong about the story she told the rat.

The door opened and William entered with a blanket which, without a word, he laid over her shoulders. He moved her chair a little closer to the fire then knelt beside her.

"How are you, Nora?" he asked.

"Fine," she said, feeling for maybe the first time that it was true. That there really was hope, that she would have her happy ever after just as Valeria had.

"You look unwell."

"No, no. Just, it's a lot. I've left a lot behind."

He looked confused. How could she explain to someone who had everything handed to him on a platter. To someone whose life was warmth and comfort. How could she ever explain that even the meagre trappings of the orphanage carried for her all the associations of something like home.

"You do not have to stay," he said looking sad. "I would not presume to dictate such a thing. However, until you are ready to leave you have employment in my house and a room of your own. I have Stephen making up one of the servants quarters for you. This house is built for a whole family and, well, I suppose the monkeys are rather like mischievous children but..."

A different sort of warmth flowed through her. She was to live under the same roof as Mister Richmond. She would work with him every day, enjoy their intimate chats and discover more about the world and his work.

"Thank you," she said. "Really, I cannot thank you enough."

William smiled. "Not a thing at all, really. I gain more by your presence than you can imagine. Besides, Stephen never seemed closer to smiling than since we brought you into our home."

She wanted to reach out and touch his face, in the little dimple where his smile went lopsided, but decorum held her back.

"I loathed that old woman for taking you away from me," he said. "And I loathe her still more for the beatings, the cold, the... the... the squalor of it all."

Nora withdrew a little at that. "Is that how you see me? Dragged up from squalor?"

"No, no. You were a flower growing in an infested bog. I have plucked you for my greenhouse, but you would be as beautiful wherever you were found. Do not doubt your value, Nora. Miss June is no judge and no God to be listened to. She has been hurt and is lashing out at those she can. I do not know how or when but it has turned her into a petty tyrant and little more."

Nora felt her cheeks blush under all these compliments, or perhaps it was the brandy.

He reached out a hand and touched her cheek, he seemed to be looking for words to express something. He had the same look when he was puzzling out some difficult chemical problem, excitement in his eyes and pleasure as well as the consternation.

Stephen came in and William stood up sharply. He turned to Stephen and Nora felt as though some great heat lamp had been turned away from her, some intense but invisible radiation.

"Look after her, Stephen. I will see you at work tomorrow, Miss Pearson, if you are well enough."

She watched him leave, thinking how gracefully he walked and wondering what it was he had been trying so hard to work out as he looked at her. He loved questions. Why? How? What is the reason? All of these made his face light up and filled his eyes with excitement. Now she realized that was how he was looking at her and the questions were hers.

Stephen took her hand and led her, still in a daze, through the kitchen and into the servants hallway. He scowled down at her. "My room is here," he said gesturing at one door. "If you need anything in the night, do not hesitate to wake me. Yours is here. There are clothes and uniforms in the wardrobe and a glass of milk and two biscuits next to the bed. Tomorrow we will get you a bath, but tonight rest."

He opened the next door in the corridor and showed her in.

Nora's jaw fell open. It was twice the size of the room where she had slept on a pallet with a dozen other girls. The room contained a bed, with a pretty pink bedspread. There was a wardrobe, a small table, and a chair all for her own use. As she looked closer she could see that the bed had fresh linen and three thick blankets atop it. On the two pillows was a clean nightgown in white cotton unstained or torn or patched up. There was a fireplace glowing nicely and a stand with a porcelain bowl of water, clean towels, and a full bar of soap.

It was the bedroom of a queen.

Without fuss he went to the bed and pulled back the covers taking a copper warming pan from the bed before pulling the blankets back. With a nod, Stephen closed the door behind her, saying, "Good night."

She tried to reply but was choking. Tears of joy fell from her face and made dark spots on the ragged orphanage dress which she would never have to wear again. She wished that little rat was here to hear it, that his story could have a happy ending too.

Washed and in a clean nightgown she climbed into the warm bed. It was so soft and luxurious and she wondered if she was in heaven. She had never felt happier, to be here, to sleep under the same roof with William. She let the tears flow freely. The last few days had been so much.

As she lay in the bed her eyes closed and she saw his face. Remembered the feeling of his touch and her hand cleaning his wounds. The fear, the hope, was all so much but now, she began to realise there was more. The future was brighter than she had ever believed and the feelings she had for William were the beginnings of love.

THE ORPHAN'S COURAGE PREVIEW

Valeria Collins squinted as the dull, grey light filtered through the filthy window. She stifled a yawn and tried to wake to another dreary morning of cold and spitting rain. It was typical of London at this time of year.

Her first thought was surprise that Miss June, the woman who ran the orphanage, hadn't made them scrub the cracked glass, with vinegar and newspaper, for at least a week. Her second was one of cold and discomfort. The wind howled through the gaps in the window and ran over her shoulder. Trying to pull the thin, dirty blanket up, she wished that Caroline would stop kneeing her in the back.

A shiver ran through her, and she huddled under the

thin blanket, inching closer to her pallet mates. Despite the fact that Caroline slept in a tight ball, at least she was warm. Lucy snuggled closer to Valeria in her sleep, snuffling in the little girl way that she had even though she was nearly eight. To one side, Nora, her best friend, looked cold and small. Her thin body shook and Valeria moved closer to her, inching the blanket over her shoulder.

Then she cuddled back down and savoured the last few minutes of rest before they were all roused from sleep. Valeria tried not to think about the day ahead of her, which would include the same never-ending drudgery that it always did. The girls would start with whatever chores Miss Jane decided to assign them for that day. Scrubbing and cleaning the house, cooking the water-thin gruel, or sweeping out the hearth were all possibilities, and she was never sure which one she dreaded the most.

Then after a bit of food, the girls would start the mending that Miss June took in so that she could earn some extra money. Valeria flexed her fingers, trying not to feel bitter about the fact that her hands always ached as did her eyes from squinting in the dim light that their paltry candles offered.

With a sigh, Valeria lifted herself off the pallet, trying not to disturb the other girls. Pulling on her tattered dress, she wondered how she would ever get adopted when she looked like a dirty waif you would find on the street. She would try to clean herself up before anyone else awoke. Sweeping her brown hair back into the ribbon she kept in her apron pocket, she decided to go outside.

Everything squeaked and creaked as she crept down the hallway to the stairs that would lead her to the kitchen. There she might be able to sneak the bucket out to the pump in the back. She knew that if Miss June caught her, she would be punished; taking the bucket to the pump was not something she was allowed to do just for herself. None of the girls were allowed to leave the building without permission. She knew that she would probably be emptying the chamber pots for the next month if she was caught. Still, she couldn't bear to go through another day so dirty and dishevelled and they only got water to wash on a Wednesday which was three days away.

As she made it to the bottom step, she heard the tell-tale clicks of low-heeled boots coming down the hallway. There was no mistaking the sound as that of Miss June.

Panic flashed through Valeria, making her heart beat so fast that it thrummed in her ears. She could not be caught. Looking around quickly, she decided to take her chances in the hall closet.

Ducking behind the door, Valeria held her breath as Miss June walked by. Only then did she realize that there was a second set of footsteps. She wondered who would be walking with Miss June this early in the morning.

"I have sent out a notice to some of our... wealthier supporters," Miss June was saying. The pair had stopped in front of the closet, so Miss June's voice echoed through the small entryway.

"What for?" Valeria recognized the voice as that of Mrs. Mulligan, the housekeeper for the wealthy widow who lived next door to the orphanage. What was she doing here this early?

Miss June sighed heavily. "We need to get some of the older orphans out of here. There have been many inquiries for placements here, so many people going to the poor house, but we do not have enough room. Not that it will stop me, but I don't think I can stand too many more brats under this roof and the older girls are more trouble. They eat more too."

"So, how many people will be coming?" Mrs. Mulligan asked.

"I'm not sure, but as many as we can get," Miss June said. "You need to try to get that employer of yours over here. The old bat would be a good benefactor. With her support, I wouldn't have to take in so much work."

Valeria tried to understand every word. The main thing that she was hearing was that she had a chance today to get adopted. It was the thing that she longed for more than anything in the world. It made her want to get cleaned up all the more. How she wished Miss June would move on. Holding her breath, she tried to imagine what it would be like to have a real home. There would be food every day and maybe even meat on a Sunday. It was a dream that put a smile on her face. This time it would be her.

After what seemed like an eternity, the two women were on their way disappearing to another part of the building.

Valeria eased out of her hiding place, and as she

stood debating whether or not now was the right time to try to get out to the pump, she heard some of the other orphans coming down the stairs. Her spirits fell. Now wasn't the right time, but she had to get cleaned up before the prospective adoptive parents came.

As Valeria headed to the kitchen area to start what she hoped would be her chores for the day—cooking was the least despicable task she could think of—she bumped right into Nora, her closest friend in the orphanage.

"Oh, Nora, sorry!" Valeria cried. "I guess I was just preoccupied."

"Is something bothering you?" Nora asked, tilting her head to one side so that her thin blond hair spilled over her shoulder.

Valeria chewed on her lower lip, and then lowering her voice, said, "I heard Miss June say that a lot of people are coming today for adoptions."

"Oh," Nora said. "That's nice."

Valeria felt the rising irritation in her chest. Nora was two years younger than she was, and sometimes in moments like this, Valeria could tell that the age gap made the younger girl slightly naive.

"I really want to get adopted," Valeria said.

Nora nodded. "I know you do, me too."

"I've been studying so hard," she said. "I found a book of poetry hidden behind the drawers in one of the attic rooms and I have been practicing my reading. And I don't know if you noticed or not, but I've been practicing my manners as well."

"You'll get adopted one day," Nora said encouragingly.

Valeria had to admire the younger girl's optimism in the face of the bleakness that surrounded them on a daily basis.

Grab The Orphan's Courage for FREE with Kindle Unlimited or just 0.99p

THANKS FOR READING

I love sharing my Victorian Romances with you and have several more waiting for my editor to approve. Join my Newsletter by clickinghere to find out when my books are available.

I want to thank you so much for reading this book, if you enjoyed it please leave a review on Amazon. It makes such a difference to me and I would be so grateful.

Thank you so much.

Sadie

Previous Books:

The Beggar's Dream

The Orphan's Courage

ABOUT THE AUTHOR

Sadie Hope was born in Preston, Lancashire, where she worked in a textile factory for many years. Married with two grown children, she would spend her nights writing stories about life in Victorian times. She loved to read all the books of this era and often found herself daydreaming of characters that would pop into her head.

She hopes you enjoy these stories for she has many more to share with you.

Follow Sadie on Facebook

Follow Sadie on Amazon

42725960R00092

Printed in Poland
by Amazon Fulfillment
Poland Sp. z o.o., Wrocław